MW01075427

THE GHOSTS OF MYSTIC SPRINGS

MYSTIC SPRINGS PARANORMAL COZY
MYSTERY SERIES: BOOK ONE

MONA MARPLE

This book was mainly written in cracks of early morning writing, only made possible by the infinite support and encouragement of my husband to go, do, write... and leave everything else to him. I am truly blessed to have a man beside me who believes in me and backs up that belief with actions that give me the time to create.

PROLOGUE: CONNIE

I finally try to give in to the migraine that's been haunting me for hours at around midnight, hours after when lights out should have been.

Jane's music isn't helping and I consider stomping across the landing to demand she turn it down, but I've been avoiding her bedroom ever since I walked in unannounced and caught her shaving her legs with my razor. It's not that I don't care, I'm just wise enough to know there are some things that girl will keep doing, and I'm better off not knowing what they are.

Mum should be home soon. She'll check on each of us, come and give me a graveyard-shift-grease kiss and whisper for me to be good, as if her warning will seep in my unconscious while I sleep. I'm not the one she needs to worry about, I want to tell her every night, but I don't, I carry on pretending to be asleep.

I've always had problems sleeping. It's not like I became a teenager and decided it'd be cool to stay up all night, like Jane. I was the baby who never slept and the child who never grew out of it. My mum's tried all the sleep training on me. I can't be cured.

The music's gone off now. She must have heard mum's key in the lock.

I squeeze my eyes closed and wait for the door to creak open, for mum's shoes to tip-tap across my carpet, but the noise doesn't come.

Instead, the house fills with silence.

Something isn't right.

I push the comforter away and turn on my bedside lamp.

I can see a light poking under my door, and Jane can't sleep with the light on. She's like a fairy tale princess with all her sleep requirements. Two and a half pillows (the other half hangs over her bed), darkness and a cup of warm milk which she would die if I told Jake Robertson about.

I knock on her door and hear a movement inside the room, but she doesn't answer me, so I push it open (little sister privilege, I'm allowed to be annoying).

My sister is cross-legged on the floor, watching herself in the mirror she bought from the neighbor's garage sale last year and has had propped against her wall ever since. And she's crying. Like, her whole face is damp.

"What's going on?" I ask, and I hear the panic in my voice and suddenly the migraine has gone, as if all I needed was more stress in my life.

Jane looks at my reflection in the mirror and it's strange how we can make eye contact like that, when we're not looking at each other, not really. *Do I understand how that works*, I wonder, but I can't remember.

"Oh Connie." She says as a big, fat tear falls off her face and lands on her clavicle. See, I know bones.

"What's happened?" I repeat.

"It's awful." Connie says, her attention still on the us in the mirror.

"Are you acting?" I ask. She's been talking about trying out for the summer play for weeks, but I haven't seen any evidence to suggest she's serious. She's still been spending her out-of-school time flicking through the magazines that Enid gives her second-hand, the best fashion choices already circled (or cut out!) and the quizzes already completed.

Jane watches herself as another tear escapes and drops onto the carpet.

"Fine, I'm not even interested." I announce, which is clearly a lie because I'm the one who got out of bed to come and ask her what had happened. To my surprise, Jane turns away from the mirror and looks at the real me.

"It's so awful." She sniffs.

"Okay..." I say, and my mind goes there. *Mom.* She should be home already, I think, even though I know there's no telling what time she'll convince the last drunk to leave so she can lock up and come home. *She's always home before dark, officer*, I remind myself of my lines. I guess we're actors already, me and Jane. "Well, you need to spill."

"Mr Raddison." She says, and I see that she's been experimenting with make-up. She has one blue eyelid and another smoky brown. The brown's better, but she'll prefer the blue. That's always the way.

"What about him?" I ask. I plop down next to her on the carpet and suddenly feel tired, like all the years of restless nights have found me, have worn me down. I don't see what our headmaster could have done to upset her so much. He doesn't even give out detentions.

"He's dead!" She exclaims, and she returns her attention

to the mirror so she can witness herself experiencing grief for the first time.

"Dead?" I ask. "Is this a joke?"

"Of course not! Who'd joke about something like that?"

"I just..." I begin. "I... why are you so upset?"

"Connie, how could you say that? He's the man in charge of our educations! Our whole teenage lives depend on him and his dimpled cheeks..."

"How did you even find this out?"

"Jake told me."

"Jake's been here?"

She nods. "He wanted to tell me himself, isn't that sweet?"

"You'd better not have let him in." I say and my eyes flit to the window, as if I might see fingerprints from where he's climbed his way inside. Sometimes I think he's only interested in my sister because we live in a ground floor flat. Easy access.

Jane shrugs. "Can you just focus? I'm not kidding, I swear, he's dead."

"Jake's probably kidding you. He hates Radish." I say with a shrug.

"Yeah, I didn't believe him either, until he started crying. It's real, I know it is. This is our whole lives ruined!"

"I don't get it..."

"You're too young to understand." Jane says. She stops crying for a moment and looks straight at the mirror-me. "What kind of education are we going to get without a headmaster?"

I can't answer that without upsetting Jane more, because I'm fairly sure Mr Raddison doesn't - didn't? - do much at all apart from lead assemblies and smile at the Year 11 girls just enough to make most of them believe he fancied them. It didn't seem like his death, if it were real, would make much of a difference at all.

"I'm sure everything will be okay." I say. A yawn slips out of my mouth. A real, live, yawn. I could punch the air but that seems a bit insensitive. "I'm going to bed, don't stay up too late. And don't worry about this, nothing's going to change."

Little did I know, everything was about to change.

**

The door bangs so hard I don't so much hear it as feel it.

It snatches me away from a sweet dream about Toby ("Tubby") Nelson finally getting revenge on the sixth form kids who have been making his life hell for years.

People always say when noises like this happen that they jump upright. I stay down, all of my body and most of my face buried under my blankets. Seems safer. I'm a lover, not a fighter.

When I hear a footstep approach, I know it's mum, because nobody else ever comes in my room in the middle of the night. Even Jane, as annoying as she is, doesn't creep around the house while people are asleep. Her strict demands around sleep have no room to fit in moonlight wanderings.

"Mum?" I whisper. Tonight, I won't pretend to be asleep, I'll let her kiss me even though she'll smell of oil and fried meats and beer. Tonight, I'll be glad to see her.

She drops herself onto my bed, and the weight of her pulls the blanket down off my face. I glance across.

And freeze.

Every part of me wants to scream, but my vocal chords refuse to work. I try to move away, to scramble out of bed, but I'm frozen in fear.

"Mr Raddison?" I ask, my voice barely a whisper.

He smiles, that dimpled smile I've seen a thousand times. He is, clearly, dead. His body is transparent, I can see my mustard-yellow curtains through him.

"Can you talk?" I ask.

He nods. "Sorry for bursting in like that. I'm getting used to how this all works."

"How all what works?"

"Well..." He says and gestures towards his ghostly self, "...this. Being a spirit."

"A spirit?"

"Ghost sounds a bit too haunted house, I think. So, how long have you been able to see us?"

"Us?"

"Spirits."

"I don't know what you mean."

"You can see me."

"Erm... yes." I say, wondering if whatever happened to Mr Raddison included a bump to the head.

"Nobody else has been able to."

"Who else have you been to?"

"Pretty much everyone." He says with a grin. "I've been busy. I decided to follow the register, alphabetical order."

"You have been busy." I say. Winters was clearly towards the end of the register.

"I'd have been busier if everyone could see me, but nobody else has. Didn't you know you could see spirits?"

I shake my head. "I must be dreaming."

"You're not."

"I must be. Jane told me you'd died, and then I got really

tired and went to sleep. I always dream about the last thing I think about."

"Lots of people do." Mr Raddison agrees. "But this isn't a dream. I can prove it."

"How?"

"I'll tell you something you couldn't have guessed, then you'll know I was here."

"Okay." I say. "Tell me how you died. I definitely didn't know that when I went to sleep."

Mr Raddison grimaces. "Ugh. Okay, it was a car accident. I drove my car into that big old cherry tree outside school. I'd been working late and I was too tired, I should have called a taxi."

"Wow." I say. I know the tree. There have been petitions to have it removed for years, it's right on a bend, hidden out of view. Lots of people have crashed into it, but they all got out of their cars and walked away. "That's too bad. Are you sad?"

"Not really." Mr Raddison says. "It was my time, I guess. I'm not in any pain, by the way."

"Oh, good." I say, feeling bad that I didn't think to check. "So, you're going to Heaven, or?"

"I don't really know what happens next." Mr Raddison said with a grin. "I'll keep popping in on the last few people on my list. Anyway, enough about me. What are you going to do next?"

I laugh at the question. "Try and go back to sleep probably."

"I mean, in life. After school."

"Oh." I say. "I'll probably get a job at the diner with my mum."

Mr Raddison shakes his head. "You could do so much more, Connie."

I shrug my shoulders. "The diner's fine."

"I have nothing against the diner." He says and points towards his stomach, which is virtually a six-pack so doesn't prove his point at all. "Or your mum. I know she works hard for you and Jane. But you're smart, very smart. I think you're University material."

I laugh, which is the only appropriate response to the idea that a Winters girl could be University material.

"I'm serious. Your grades are good enough."

"It's not about the grades."

"What is it about?" He asks.

I gesture to the room and suddenly feel embarrassed that Mr Raddison, even if he is dead, is in our little flat. The carpet has worn away in places, flashing the floorboards below, and the walls are still covered in pen marks from the people who were here before us. Mum's always saving, but there's too much month at the end of the money. Jane and I could repeat that sentence in our sleep, we hear it so often. Mum opening the cupboards in the kitchen frantically, bang, bang, bang, then appearing in the living room with a smile. *I'm not even that hungry tonight, how about you guys?*

"That's not my world." I say.

"Well, I think it could be." Mr Raddison says, and gets up, giving me chance to notice that he has no feet. His body ends in a wisp where his legs should be. "Give it some thought."

He evaporates away and I pinch my arm until I draw blood.

1

CONNIE

"Absolutely not." I say for the third time. My hands are at that stage where they resemble wrinkled sultanas, but I'm staying in the bath to avoid being mobbed. I slide down underneath the water and close my eyes, enjoying a moment's peace, and then as always I feel guilty and reemerge from my watery hiding place.

"You're so mean." Sage says with a pout.

"I'm the one who has to think sensibly." I say. "It would be a disaster."

"It could help bring the community together."

"The community is together enough already." I say, but she's smart, she's found my weak spot.

"I just think it would be fun." Sage says.

I sigh in her general direction. She's sat on the toilet, the lid down thankfully, the way she has done since we were in our late teens and moved out together into a shared flat. My sister may have changed her name, but she's remained the same in virtually every other way.

"I'll think about it." I say.

"Yay!" She exclaims, and I've always been a soft touch

when it comes to making her happy, so her delight pretty much seals the deal. There will be a party.

"You'll have to help, you know." I say, then add: "If I agree."

"Of course." Sage says. A flower tiara sits atop her head.

"I mean, really help. Not just flit around looking busy."

"Your problem, sis, is you're a control freak. You want help but nobody does it as good as you, so you don't let people help." Sage says with an infuriating grin. She's right, of course.

"Can I just have this bath in peace?" I ask. "It's been a long week."

Sage makes a mock salute and pretends to zip her mouth closed, but makes no effort to move. I feel like a mother of small children, every bath time or toilet visit interrupted.

I do love her, though. I can't deny that.

I watch her as she sits there, staring straight ahead, lips pursed inwards so I know she's still making a point of being quiet.

I slide back down under the water and visualise the stresses and tension leaving my body. I saw the technique in a magazine, help for busy people, but haven't had the time to try it.

I close my eyes and think back to the client meetings of the last week; eight when I've said for years my limit is five. One a day is tiring, any more becomes exhausting. And I'm not a fun person to be around when I'm exhausted. I get snappy. And my eye starts to twitch in a creepy way.

I must be more strict. No matter how desperate people are to see me, my limit has to be five meetings a week.

It's all urgent, of course, that's the problem. Nobody wants to join a waiting list. They want to come now, today, and if I can't do that, they'll find someone unscrupulous who can.

Five meetings a week. I force myself to focus on those words, repeat them silently until I imagine they've sunk into my unconscious. Sage is all about the unconscious. Always banging on about your inner mind and the guidance system it can offer.

I feel my shoulders begin to relax and slide up so my nose, and only my nose, is above the surface of the water. Okay, okay, my stomach is too. Nothing I can do about that one, thank you very much.

I begin to picture the party that Sage wants me to throw. It seems like such an obviously bad idea, and yet I know it will happen. I can't hold up against Sage's ongoing begging campaign.

An April Fools' party! It will be so much fun.

And who am I to say no to fun? Only the person who'll have to do all of the non-fun parts so that other people can turn up to enjoy the fun itself.

My shoulders are tensing again.

I return to the visualisation technique before giving up. If my life means I can last two minutes without the tension returning, I might be better off to just accept it. Live with it. Isn't there a quote about how being wise is knowing which things you can change and which you can't? If not, there should be. Because I'm definitely realising that accepting the chaos that is my life may be my best option.

I push my body above the water and enjoy the silence.

When I open my eyes, I see that Sage has gone, and I feel the pang I do every time she leaves. *Will she come back?*

I drain the water and sit in the empty tub for a few moments, which I don't recommend you do if you're blessed with a body like mine. It's impossible not to question whether you might actually be part beached-whale, which hardly starts the day on a good note.

Getting dry is one of life's jobs that I refuse to play any active role in, so I wrap a towel around me and walk across to my bedroom, where I lie myself down on the bed and pick up the mystery novel I've been trying to work through for almost a month. My morning routine always gives enough time for nature to dry me, and I will remain here until that has happened.

It's been so long since I picked up the book that I can't remember who Bill or Sarah-Anne are, or why they were in the church alone in the first place. I sigh and return my bookmark (a cute photo of me and Sage, back when she was Jane, in dreadful clothes and toothy grins) to page one.

Time to begin again.

But no time to begin again, as I note the familiar presence appear in the doorway.

"Shall I tell Atticus it's on, then? The party?"

"Okay." I say with a sigh, returning the book to the bedside table.

Sage grins and does a girlish twirl, so I roll my eyes. "Shall we have a theme? Ooh, I know, fancy dress! I love fancy dress."

"You're really not the event planner in the family, are you?" I ask. "First of all, we need to pick a venue."

"That's easy." Sage says with a shrug. "The Baker house."

"The Baker house?" I repeat. "I don't think that's a good idea."

"You pick somewhere then." Sage says, carefree. This is how she gets me. She makes one ridiculous suggestion that clearly can't work, and then when I say no, she opts out of any other work. On the basis that she tried to help and I wouldn't let her. Well, I can beat her at her own game.

"Let's give the Baker house a go." I say and jump up from the bed. I'm dry enough. I pull on knickers that shock me every time I wear them. Big, grey granny pants that I don't remember buying, that I'd never want another person to see, but that I keep washing and wearing because they're so comfortable. I'm aware of Sage watching and I can imagine how disappointed she must be to have a sister who wears knickers like these. She's a big fan of teeny-weeny underwear. I'm a teeny-weeny fan of big underwear.

"Are you going to tell Atticus?" Sage asks.

"Yes, if I see him." I say. Atticus, the former mayor of Mystic Springs, still tries to run the town. There's no new mayor to do the job. No police either.

"Oh, I'm sure you will. Where are you going?" Sage asks.

"For a walk." I say. "Alone."

Sage laughs. "I know when I'm not wanted."

"I just need some quiet time." I say. "I won't be long."

The familiar fear rears its ugly head. *Will she still be here?*

"You could come... if you want." I say, the vision of a peaceful walk disappearing as the words leave my mouth.

She raises her shoulder up to her chin in a slow, drawn-out shrug. "I've got other things to do."

"What other things?" I ask, transformed from the sister who wanted to be alone to the sister who doesn't. Sage can play me like a violin.

"Oh, I'm kidding." She says with a syrupy laugh. "I'll walk with you if you want."

She infuriates me, she drives me insane, but she's my best friend.

And I'm so lucky to have this second chance with her.

So I grin and pull a brightly coloured blouse over my head. I've got two hours before my client meeting, and the walk is a daily ritual to clear my head before I see anyone.

I'm usually up and out before Sage wakes up, but the excitement of the April Fools' party has apparently left her needing no sleep. I could hear her banging around the house all through the night while I tried, in vain, to get the elusive eight hours everyone else seems to take for granted.

Maybe a walk will tire her out, I think, as if she's a small child or an overexcited puppy.

"Come on then." I say.

We walk aimlessly from my house on the outskirts of Mystic Springs into the town itself. It's a strange place, with a small population but a heavy tourist presence. Atticus Hornblower, the ex-mayor, saw the town's dwindling economy and decided to begin a genius marketing campaign suggesting that the natural water springs that the town is named after had healing properties. There was absolutely no truth in it, but desperate people want to believe, and so they started arriving in droves to bathe their eczema-wrecked feet, to trickle the water over their breaking hearts, to even wash their hair here with shampoo to try and get rid of grey.

The good times lasted for a while, until the national authorities heard about the claims and came to shut us down. Apparently, you can't just pretend your waterfall can cure disease. But a funny thing happened. Everyone the authorities spoke to were adamant they had been cured by the springs.

Maybe this town had the last laugh.

And so, Mystic Springs is now one of the most popular tourist destinations for people seeking complementary therapies, that's the way we have to describe it.

I follow the route I usually take on these morning walks, heading for the waterfall. I like to stand and watch the water flow for ten minutes, it clears my mind, prepares me for the day ahead. For my work.

I see Lola Anti standing ahead, watching the water. I feel my stomach sink. This is meant to be my alone time. Nobody else is at the springs this early, usually.

"Good morning." I call.

Lola is a small young woman with unkempt brown hair. She turns at the sound of my voice and looks as disappointed to see me as I was to see her.

"Hi." She says, then returns her attention to the springs.

"Nice day for a walk." I say, thinking that if I annoy her enough, she might leave.

She doesn't reply.

I glance towards Sage and roll my eyes, then drop my weight onto a bench overlooking the water. I'll have to just ignore them both.

"I might go for a wander." Sage says, fidgety by my side.

"Okay." I say. "I've got a client at 10am, remember."

"I know." Sage says. She has to stay out of the way when I have a meeting, that's the only rule I have that's non-negotiable, and she follows it. I'm sure she's sometimes sat on the other side of the door, listening, but as long as she's quiet - and invisible - I'm prepared to let that go.

"Have a good day, Connie." Lola calls across to me as she turns on her heels and walks away from the springs. She doesn't wait for a reply before walking away and, as always with Lola, I'm left wondering if I'm the butt of some joke I'm not cool enough to understand.

"How rude." Sage says. It's one of her favourite jokes, now completely overused and predictable.

Of course Lola wouldn't say goodbye to my sister.

She can't see ghosts.

2

SAGE

I know my sister thinks I'm a total bore with the jokes about people ignoring me, but it's not entirely meant to be funny.

It's pretty strange to be ignored day after day after day by people who I can see clearly.

Sometimes I forget they can't see me, and I get actually offended.

Funny, huh?

Who said ghosts don't have feelings?

Anyway, it's clear Connie is zoned out watching the waterfall, so I come away for a walk on my own.

Shall we get the questions out of the way first?

No, I don't exactly walk, it's more floating. Ghosts don't have feet, our spirit energy ends in a kind of wispy tail, I guess. Other than that, I look a little shaky, like a photo that won't quite focus, but I still have my face and I look like me. I haven't turned into a cartoon ghost, okay.

So, when you're picturing me, the best thing to focus on is my incredible beauty, right, not my ghostliness.

Ha! I'm kidding, but please do feel free to picture me as incredibly beautiful. Artistic licence, and all that.

Mystic Springs is dead at this time of morning - no pun intended. The school kids are still at home panic-finishing homework if they're anything like I was at their age, and the workers? Well, let's just say that Mystic Springs isn't the kind of town where people are breaking their backs working. It's more about clocking off early and firing up the grill than clocking up 14 hour shifts in an office cubicle. Which is probably why the town struggled so much financially before the magical healing waters were invented.

I like it here, though. I call it home now, even though I can move around wherever I want (a bonus of being dead).

The scenery is pretty epic, for a hippie-at-heart like me. I always dreamed of big, wide open places, and this is it.

If you're wondering about me being lonely, don't. I can see and talk to anyone in the spirit world, and my sister in the human world.

And, I know there's going to be one ghoulish person wondering how I died. It's you, isn't it? Well, let me stop you. I don't know. I don't remember. That's pretty unusual, but I'm not going to be going to any ghost therapy to work it all out, okay. So, It's just an unknown. Like why my sister wears those huge knickers. And yes, of course, I could just ask her - about my death and the knickers - but really, I don't want either conversation.

"Leave me alone, you silly little girl." Someone shouts up ahead. I speed up, because I love a good argument. Stood in her garden, I see Nettie Frasier, the most attractive woman in the town if you ask me. She's all 1950s glamour, it's insane. She's dressed down in super-cute denim dungarees, a small shovel in her hand, but her lips are her trademark red as always.

"Silly little girl? That's not what your husband called me." It's Lola Anti who shouts this in her sing-song voice and her words make me wince. We've all heard the rumours. Desmond Frasier, investment banker with a capital W, and recent member of the Dead Club, had steak at home and was going out for cheap burgers.

"My husband was a fool." Nettie says. I get so close I can see the beads of sweat on her forehead, she must have been out here some time working on her borders. "You're just a silly kid."

"I pleased him in ways you couldn't." Lola says. She's on the other side of the white picket fence, Nettie could just go back into her house and close the front door. Lock this mean girl out. But she won't. Nettie won't let Lola have the last word.

"You know what?" Nettie asks, red lips pursed. "You two deserved each other."

"He was going to leave you." Lola sings.

"Rubbish." Nettie says with a laugh. "He told you all that. You're not the first girl he's had an affair with, you know. And you wouldn't have been the last if he hadn't died."

"Maybe you should ask why you couldn't keep him happy at home, then." Lola says. She leans over the fence, sees the glare on Nettie's face, and steps back again.

"And maybe you should ask why you'd want to be with a married man twice your age." Nettie says.

Oh no, I think. Because there's only one answer, and it's so obvious.

"I followed the money, honey." Lola sings, and as she does, she looks past Nettie to the grand house that stands behind her. It's a traditional plantation house with wrap-around balconies on the first and second floors, and a perfectly manicured lawn. A single, heavy wooden rocking chair sits on the first floor veranda next to a coffee table where Nettie often leaves her book, sunglasses and a glass of lemonade. There were two rocking chairs, before. I watched her drag the second one across town to the tip after she found out about the affair.

She tells the story sometimes, the night her strength was so super human she pulled a rocking chair across town. She doesn't know I had hold of the other end of it, sharing the weight with her. I had to rest for three days afterwards.

I can touch things, but it drains me, and it took practice.

I've been dead a long time.

"Well, that's no surprise." Nettie says.

"We're the same really." Lola sings. "You're set up now, aren't you? The big house, the money... you could say we're both gold diggers."

A shiver runs through me then and I feel my stomach fill with dread. Something has changed. I look from Lola to Nettie, but it's not them.

And then I see him. Desmond.

If you picture what an investment banker who had routine affairs would look like, you'll be picturing Desmond.

He's on her rocking chair, which he knows she would hate, and he's watching. Just watching the two women argue, over him, over his mistakes, over his money. It's clear which he is concerned by.

When he died, Nettie had to take on a huge legal battle for her share of his estate. He'd tried to leave everything; the house, the cars, the money, in Trust for his second life. Desmond is a believer that those wealthy enough to freeze their bodies, as he of course did, will be brought back to life in the future. Personally, I can't imagine anything worse. Who knows what kind of state you might return to?

"I'm nothing like you." Nettie says, her voice calm and clear. "I'm worth a hundred of you."

"Keep telling yourself that." Lola says. "But we both know I should have had some of all, all this."

"You had enough of his money when he was alive." Nettie says.

"You just want to keep it all for yourself. You played the long game, waiting for him to die." Lola says. "In fact..."

"I'm bored of you now." Nettie says, swatting towards Lola with a long, slender hand.

Lola grins at her and raises her voice. "How did he die, Nettie? Are we sure it was an accident?"

Nettie's cheeks flush. The town is getting busier now and neighbours are piling kids into cars. A few people glance towards the commotion at the sound of Lola's raised voice.

"Maybe he was pushed." Lola shouts. "But who would want him dead?"

Nettie shakes her head. "You're unbelievable."

"Remind me, who was there when he fell down the stairs? Oh, just you! And what were you doing before the fall? I remember, you were arguing..." Lola sings, as she leans in close to Nettie. "Arguing about me. Maybe he told you he was going to leave you? Maybe you got scared of being left with no husband, and no money... how embarrassing. Did he scream when you pushed him?"

Nettie slaps Lola across the face with such force the echo of the crack seems to reverberate from the nearby mountains. Both women gasp and step backwards, Nettie covers her mouth and Lola breaks into a grin.

"Ah, now we're seeing the real you." She says, then turns towards the nearest neighbour, who stands mouth agape by his car. "Did you see that? Can I take your details so you can be a witness, I'd like to press charges."

Nettie groans and sinks back into the grass behind her fence. Her cheeks are as flush as her lips.

Desmond laughs from the rocking chair, a sound that only other spirits, and Connie, would be able to hear. He picks up Nettie's book and moves the bookmark to a different page, then vanishes.

I breathe deeply once he was gone; the air feels cleaner, more fresh.

I leave Nettie gazing dumbly into the flower beds.

Despite what Connie says, this town needs a party.

I float across town to the Baker house, the large, abandoned mansion where most of the town's spirits gather. It's the perfect place for a party that will bring together the living and the spirits, because the people of Mystic Springs have been complaining about the parties at the Baker house for decades, even though it's been empty for twenty years. Most people in the town have walked past after dark and heard loud music playing, or people laughing, or even seen shapes moving behind the curtains.

My belief is that most people don't see ghosts because they don't believe in them.

A party in the Baker house could be out of town kids, squatters, or any number of other logical explanations, so people let themselves see and hear what's going on in there. Luckily, Mystic Springs has no police force, so the parties never get shut down.

Because, trust me, the parties here are out of this world.

I let myself in and crash on the settee next to Atticus. It was such a blow to the town when he died, horse riding accident, far too young. He's a thoughtful, creative man with a kind heart and narrow framed glasses.

"How's the party planning?" He asks.

I hadn't exactly admitted that Connie was against the

idea. Look, I know my sister and I know how to wear her down. It was always going to be a yes, it was just a question of how long she pretended it was going to be a no.

"Connie's working on it." I say. It's quiet in the house, the grand living room is empty apart from me and Atticus. "I've just seen a huge argument."

"Hmm?" Atticus asks, attention piqued in his subtle way.

"Lola and Nettie."

"Oh, Lord. Won't she leave that poor woman alone?"

"I know." I agree. Nettie is universally liked. Lola, on the other hand, arrived in town as a runaway who'd ran out of cash and needed to find money quick, which she did in the shape of Desmond Frasier. "Lola was pretty vile to her. She suggested that Nettie had pushed Desmond down the stairs."

Atticus looks at me with concern. "What did Nettie say?"

"Well..." I stumble, not wanting to admit that Nettie had hit Lola. "She didn't really say anything."

"I guess she was lucky there's no police here. It would have been investigated, if there had been."

"What, really?"

"Of course. It was pretty suspicious how he fell just after she'd found out about the affair."

I'd never considered that.

"Nettie's so nice, though."

"Hell hath no fury..." Atticus said, then broke into a grin. "Anyway, back to April Fools. The first party ever for both spirits and the living. This could open up a whole new income stream for Mystic Springs, you know. Imagine how many people would like to celebrate with their dead loved ones!"

3

CONNIE

*W*eeks of planning.

Alright, a week and a half.

The invitations had come from me, of course. As the town's medium, I had to be the one to appear to suggest it.

A party for the living and the dead!

Come and party with the dead!

In the end, I called it Ghosts and Fools. Which was not ideal, because it seemed to suggest that the living people were fools.

Luckily, most of them were too foolish to consider the invitation in that much detail.

"Are you wearing that?" Sage asks, appearing in the bedroom doorway.

"I wish you'd knock." I say. I'm grumpy because I'm trying on clothes. There are people in the world - my sister was one of them - who find trying on clothes to be fun. A hobby. And then there are people like me, who have to tuck their stomachs into their knickers and hope for the best. "What's wrong with it, anyway?"

Sage looks me up and down before giving an eye roll, as

if I'm too far gone for help, which may very well be true. "Wear the black."

"Black? It's not a funeral." I say. The four outfits that were the least bad had formed a shortlist and were each laid out on my bed.

"I guess." Sage says. "Wear what you want, then."

I look at my reflection. I'm wearing a shapeless tent of a dress which somehow is so baggy that you can't even be sure I have a stomach, while still managing to make me look more fat than I am.

"Everyone makes the same mistake." Sage says. "Tries to hide the bits they don't like with baggy clothes, but it's not flattering. Wear the black, it's more fitted, and you can wear that lilac scarf to add some colour."

I sigh and pull the tent over my head, replacing it with the black number, that I have to wiggle into. It shows my stomach, but I get what Sage means. There's an honesty to it. At least it doesn't make me look like a fat person who's trying to pretend she's not fat.

I should say here, I don't mind being overweight. In the competition between exercising and cake, I choose cake every time, and I'm not really worried about that. I'm happy in my skin. I just find choosing clothes stressful.

And being surrounded by my dead sister doesn't help. She died when her metabolism could still work miracles.

"That's lovely." Sage says, and I have to agree. I toss the tent dress out into the hallway so I remember to send it to a charity shop instead of returning it to the plus-sized sanctuary that is my wardrobe.

"Does everyone know the rules for tonight?" I ask.

"Of course." Sage says, but she's looking at her own reflection in the mirror and I can tell I've lost her attention.

"I really want this to go well." I say. "Well, I need it to. I'll be blamed if anyone acts up."

"Mm-hmm." Sage replies as she licks her lips and puckers up for a pout.

I sigh. "Come on, let's go."

We walk across town and hear the music even before the Baker house comes into view. I've spent the last two days cleaning the house from top to bottom, scrubbing floors, wiping down dusty woodwork. I left a few cobwebs for effect and held a spontaneous meeting with the spirits who just happened to be there, playing solitaire, to explain how everyone needed to be on best behaviour.

They'd all looked at me wide-eyed, of course, as if they don't live for pranks.

The house is full, and the sight that greets me is overwhelming. Living people, dancing next to spirits they can't see. Spirits, very able to see the living people, dancing next to the ones they loved or had taken a liking to. It takes me a moment to get my bearings, to be able to focus in and see who's alive and who's dead.

To my amusement, Atticus is dancing in between his daughter Mariam and her friend and colleague Desiree. His ghostly form gazes at his daughter with such love that I realise in that moment that the party is a good idea. Mariam has struggled since her father's sudden death, and I subtly check the glass in her hand and note with relief that it contains orange juice.

"This is amazing!" Sage squeals and I laugh. "I'm going to go and work the room."

Of course she is.

I smile to myself and walk across to Violet Warren, the town battleaxe. In a leopard print mini-dress, dangling rainbow earrings and with neon highlights in her white fringe, she looks pretty much the same as she does any other day. She sees me and pulls me in for a hug.

"Connie! What an amazing idea." She calls. Her age is anyone's guess, but she's my senior and yet has more energy and excitement for life than I've ever had.

"Is it going well?" I ask.

"It's fabulous! When will the spooks make an appearance?" Violet asks. Never married, and child free, Violet has never come to me for an appointment, and I'm not sure whether she believes in the spirit world or not.

"They're already here." I say, casting a glance towards Patton Davey, whose ghostly form stands in police uniform with a baton in his hand. Never off duty, even in death, he says, which is just as well as he was never replaced after he died.

"Oh, tremendous." Violet says with a laugh. "Atticus Hornblower owes me ten dollars still, so tell me if he pops in."

I laugh. Atticus has heard her and flashes a mischievous grin, then rushes at speed towards Violet, floating right through her. She grabs her stomach instinctively.

"Ooh, I feel funny." She says.

I cast a warning glance towards Atticus, but it's too late. The other spirits have seen his trick and decide to join in.

"April Fools!" One spirit calls, then zips through the body of Desiree Montag, the school principal. Desiree drops her glass to the floor and grabs her stomach.

"Is it the shrimp?" Someone calls.

I manage to meet Sage's gaze and flash her a warning look.

"Guys, come on, tone it down a bit." Sage calls, but authority was never her strong point and nobody listens to her.

"I thought this was a party?" I shout,as I head over to the ancient speakers to turn up the volume. "Let's dance!"

My distraction works and most people grab a partner and strut their stuff. I join in, enjoying the party as much as I can while remaining on low alert. I've never brought my two worlds together in such a way, inviting the spirits to spend an extended period with the living inhabitants of Mystic Springs.

Most people imagine spirits to be sombre, permanently upset about their death and stuck in a limbo between the real world and the after life. That's not how it works. People generally stay the same after death.

Lots of my customers want to come and connect with a loved one who has passed, and all they want to do is talk about how awful it is that that person has died, and how they died, and how wrong it all is. The spirit will be so bored by this they might refuse to stick around for the whole of the appointment.

Death is a moment.

The dead have experienced it and generally want to move on.

I grab Violet and try to imitate her wacky dance moves, but I'm more self-conscious than she is (heck, who isn't). She keeps my pace, then speeds up and laughs as my face grows red. When I start to actually pant and see stars in my vision, I know it's time to grab a drink and have a seat.

In the kitchen, Lola Anti sits astride the counters, mobile phone in hand, texting furiously.

"Enjoying the party?" I ask as I grab a glass and fill it with iced tea.

She shrugs without taking her attention from her phone. She's such a pretty girl.

I take my glass and turn to leave the kitchen, when I spot Troy Montag standing alone, watching Lola.

"Hey, you okay?" I ask.

Troy nods. "Yes, ma'am. Great party."

I grin. "Not dancing?"

Troy laughs. "Nah, I was born in the wrong skin colour."

I laugh. Troy is a good kid, a philosophy student with a trimmed black Afro and impeccable manners.

"Do you think she's ok in there?" I ask, gesturing back towards Lola with a twist of my head.

"She? Oh, erm..." He stammers, coffee-coloured cheeks staining pink.

"Oh, you didn't see? Lola's in there all alone. Do you two know each other?"

"Oh. Yeah, I know who she is." Troy says. I'm pretty sure all boys his age know who she is. "I don't know her enough to go up and talk to, though, ma'am, sorry."

"I'm sure she's fine, just lost on her phone." I say with a wink. I don't want him to feel uncomfortable. As the principal's son, it's no secret that as soon as he can, he's leaving Mystic Springs in search of a city where he can join the faceless masses.

"I do that too sometimes." He says. "It helps if I'm feeling a little shy, just to hide away on my own for a bit, check in online."

"Hmm, is that right?" I say. I can't imagine Lola Anti ever feeling shy. The girl seems to attract drama and pain wherever she goes. "Well, I'm going to sit down for a bit. Violet's worn me out."

"She'll do that." Troy says with an easy smile. I hope he doesn't leave, I think suddenly, and with such urgency I almost say it out loud. I shake my head to push the thought away. I have very little to do with Troy - he is a teenage boy, after all - and yet every time I do speak to him, I feel a connection.

I find an empty seat on a big leather reclining settee which once would have been the focal point of the room and now sits tattered and sags under the weight of anyone who collapses into it. Time and age will do that, I think, make us all tattered and saggy. I snort a little at my own weak joke and am pleased nobody is close enough to have noticed.

The party is winding down. The spirits are restless, I can feel it. The humans have come, eaten, drank, danced, but they haven't seen a single spirit. They were never going to, of course, hosting a party isn't all it takes to give a person the powers to see spirits, but it's clear the party has left both sides confused. The whooshing noise of spirits floating through people brings me back to full attention.

Mariam Hornblower looks green as she clutches her stomach.

"Is it something you ate?" Desiree asks. "I heard someone mention the shrimp earlier."

"It's fine." I say, as Mariam throws up over the floor.

"Enough!" Atticus roars, the fun and games over now his own daughter is ill, even though he was the spirit who started the pranks.

Mariam bends over and clasps her stomach, Desiree at her side.

"Are you okay?" Desiree asks. "Can we get some water?"

"No." Mariam objects. "I don't want anything else from in here. Can you take me home?"

Desiree is about to answer when a piercing scream comes from the kitchen.

I jump off the settee, silently vowing never to host a dead or alive party again, and race in to the kitchen.

"Is she...?" Violet asks, her face ashen.

I peer over the crowd who managed to race towards the noise quicker than I did, and manage to make out the lifeless shape on the floor. A knife protruding from her back, mobile phone still in hand. Lola Anti.

4

SAGE

We've taken up residence in Connie's attic, which she doesn't exactly know about, but she can hardly argue it. Nobody wants to be in the Baker house right now.

I know she feels guilty about a person being killed at a party she organised, but it's really not her fault. She didn't kill Lola.

I've tried to tell her that but she's being pretty tight-lipped about everything.

Patton Davey has called this meeting urgently, and he never calls meetings. When I get told there's another meeting being led by Atticus, I'm already bored before I've even arrived. I mean, he's a great person, but he loves to create a meeting where one isn't needed.

So, a meeting with Patton, that's something to get interested in.

Patton Davey is the definition of an Alpha male. He can take control of a situation with a look. And he's super nice to look at, which is why I take the seat opposite him for the meeting. Even if the meeting itself turns out to be snoretastic, I can sit back and look at his chiselled jaw and icy blue eyes.

Atticus is here, of course, but nobody else.

Just the three of us. Interesting.

Patton floats in, in his Sheriff's uniform of course, and clears his throat.

"Thanks for coming." He says, looking at each of us in turn which takes no time at all because there's just me and Atticus. "We need to talk about Lola."

"Kevin." I say, unable to stop the weak book-title joke slipping out of my mouth. Patton glances at me, coughs again, and then focuses his attention on Atticus, probably rethinking my invitation.

"It's an awful business." Atticus says, his gaze down towards his lap.

"We need to investigate." Patton says. "We have a murderer in Mystic Springs and we have to catch them."

"Won't they send out a police force from another town?" I ask.

Patton shook his head. "I used to get calls to help out in other towns, and trust me, those requests went to the bottom of my to do list. Or the shredder. Nobody's got time to pick up another town's work."

"But a murder." Atticus said, stroking his white bristle of a beard. "Surely, that calls for action."

"Yes, sir. It calls for action by us."

"What can we do?"

"We can listen." Patton says. "We can be in the right place, at the right time, and hear something that will solve the case."

"So you want us to basically spy on people for gossip? I'm in." I say with a clap of my hands. Patton eyes me.

"This isn't a game." He scolds me.

"I know that." I say, defensive. Although I have no belief in whether a group of ghosts can solve a murder, so it sounds pretty like a game to me.

"Do you have any suspects?"

"At this stage, we need to gather intel." Patton says. "It's too soon to be talking suspects."

"What do you want us to do?" Atticus asks. "And, I'm guessing this is to be kept between us?"

"Absolutely. This is an investigation, it has to remain private. Can you do that?" Patton asks, and it's me he looks at.

"Of course I can." I say defensively, although keeping secrets has never been my strong point.

"Atticus, I need you to watch and listen. You know the people, you know how they act and if something's wrong. I need you to gather info for me."

"And me too?" I ask. I'm giddy with excitement at the thought of being head hunted for a Sheriff's investigation, even if the Sheriff is dead.

"Oh no." Patton says. "I don't want you to do anything Sage, but I need your sister's help, and I know she'll agree if you ask her."

"That's it?" I ask.

"Connie can interrogate our suspects, when we have them. We can't do this without a living person."

"Well, you can ask her yourself." I say, petulant. Connie always says I'm great at sulking. Let's see.

"She barely knows me." Patton says. That's true. When he was alive, Patton was one of the most vocal in terms of suggesting that Connie's gift was a hoax, that there was no such thing as ghosts, and that she was basically a charlatan for taking money from vulnerable, grieving people. He's never quite been able to look her in the eye since he died.

"I'm not going to ask her for you, and then sit out and have nothing to do with this investigation." I say. There. My cards are laid out on the table. Your move, Sheriff.

He sighs. "What do you want to do?"

"I want to help." I admit, and then my mind flashes back to the argument, to the slap that Nettie planted across Lola's face. "And I'm pretty sure I have information you'll want."

"She does." Atticus says with a slow nod of his head, clearly thinking of the same incident.

"Your first job is to convince Connie to be on board. Do that, and then we can talk." Patton says. His walkie talkie springs into life then, static and then a voice, a call for back up. He switches it off and rolls his eyes. "Damn thing picks up calls from all over the state. Do we have a deal?"

"Sure." I say. "I'll speak to my sister."

"Okay. Let's meet back here same time tomorrow, with Connie too. If she's here, you can have some investigative work to do Sage, if she isn't, there's no point you coming. Meeting dismissed."

Patton fades away and Atticus looks across at me.

"He's a fine Sheriff."

"I said nothing." I protest, but Atticus gives me a knowing look.

"He'll get the job done. And that's what we need. A murderer on the loose will be awful for business."

**

Connie is baking, and the kitchen is in a fine mess.

It's as if she gets the flour and throws it across the room in some strange worship ritual to the Gods of baked goods.

I take a seat at the big oak table and wait for her to notice my presence, something she's surprisingly bad at for a medium.

Finally, she pours the mixture into a cake tin and places it in the oven, then sets a timer and spins on her heels.

"Sage, for goodness sake, stop creeping up on me." She says, clutching her hand to her chest.

"Sorry." I say.

"There's a murderer in town and I've got people sneaking up on me, it's not good for my health." She says, collapsing into the chair across from me.

"What's cookin'?" I ask.

"Banana loaf, hopefully." She says. "I didn't have all the ingredients, but I needed something to do."

"Has Lola come to see you yet?"

Connie's eyes widen and she shakes her head. She's had a few murder victims over the years but generally she dislikes them. The relatives are always so emotional, and the spirits can be angry and challenging too.

"You don't want her to?"

"There's no reason for her to see me, we weren't close." Connie says. "And she's got no family here."

"Or friends." I say.

Connie raises an eyebrow. The kitchen begins to fill with the aroma of sweet banana and spiny cinnamon, and Connie pushes herself up to her feet and grabs a damp cloth. She wipes the flour and globs of cake mixture from the table then turns her attention to the counters, all coated with pieces of egg shell and splashes of milk.

I sit back and watch, enjoying the light seeping in the window by the sink. My lack of activity doesn't go unnoticed, I realise, from the heavy sighs Connie makes as she opens the bin and empties the eggshell in.

"You could help, you know." She mutters.

"I've been very busy today, actually." I say with a smile and a flick of my hair.

"Oh really? Doing what?"

"I was called to a meeting."

She's curious now. She rinses the cloth and then turns to face me.

"The Sheriff's putting together a team to investigate the murder." I say with a casual shrug.

"And you're on it?" Connie asks, then cringes. "Sorry, I didn't mean it to come out like that."

"Me and Atticus, that's it." I say.

"Small team." She quips as she fills the kettle and sets it to boil, then empties the dishwasher, leaving her favourite cup on the side ready to refill.

"Patton doesn't want too many people involved, it's all very hush-hush."

"And yet you're telling me." Connie says with a murmur. "What do you want, Sage?"

I let out a high-pitched giggle and roll my eyes. "I'm just proud to have been asked and I wanted my little sister to know."

Connie eyes me as she spoons coffee into her cup. "Really?"

"Of course." I say. "It feels like I'm finally being accepted here."

"You've always been accepted." Connie says. "Everywhere you go, people love you. It's always been like that."

I shrug. "It doesn't feel like I'm taken seriously sometimes."

"Well, I'm pleased you're happy about this. It'll be nice for you to have something to focus on."

"Yep." I say. "It's going to take up a lot of time, I might not see you as much."

"That's fine. You know where I am when you can fit me in your busy schedule." Connie says with an easy smile.

"You could help me." I say, my eyes wide as if the idea has just hit me.

"Me?" Connie says with a laugh. "I've got enough going on, thanks."

"Oh... I just thought you might like to have something for us to do together."

Connie fills her cup with steaming hot water and takes a sip, then curses the hot liquid and returns the cup to the counter. She does the same thing most days. "You'll be great at this, you don't need me."

"I know I don't need you." I lie. "I just wanted you to be involved. Patton says we need one living person, and I fought your corner so he'd consider it being you."

"You fought my corner?"

"You know what he's like, all that charlatan stuff..." I say, my voice fading away.

"Which is clearly false, since I see him around town avoiding me."

"I know, I know... men." I say with raised eyebrows. "But anyway, this would be such a fun thing for us to do together."

"I don't think investigating a murder will be fun, Sage. Are you sure you've thought this through?"

"Yes mum!" I whine. "I meant us being together, that bit would be fun. "Please?"

Connie shakes her head. "I'm quite happy without that extra stress in my life. It's sweet that you thought of me, and I agree it would be nice to do more together, but not this, okay?"

"Connie, your town needs you." I say in mock seriousness.

She laughs and swats at me with her chubby fingers. "My town is in serious trouble if I'm the best hope it's got. Why don't you ask Violet, she knows everything."

"She can't..."

"Oh, yeah! You can't ask her." Connie says with a laugh. She picks up her coffee cup and walks across the kitchen, then pauses in the doorway and looks at me with a pointed expression. "I can see right through you Sage, in more ways than one. You need a person who can speak to you spirits, and I'm the only option. Well, it's a no. I'm sorry. Lola's murder has reminded me how much I want a nice quiet life. You'll have to solve this without me... or leave it to the police."

"The police aren't coming." I say, weakly, as she leaves the room.

5

CONNIE

*T*he Mystic Springs Town Board have called a meeting and made it clear that no excuse is good enough to not attend.

All across town people are changing work shifts, closing businesses early, and ringing in sick for out-of-town jobs.

When I arrive, just a few minutes before the stroke of seven, and slightly out of breath because I decided to walk over without really having enough time, there's a queue outside the Town Hall.

The Town Hall is mainly used for community events. Mystic Springs is big on community. We've had street parties for celebrity weddings, afternoon tea for the British Royal Wedding, and of course this place goes wild for Hallowe'en.

But an actual, come and sit down, meeting? Never happens.

In large part, that could be down to the hole that's been left in the town since the mayor and the sheriff are dead. Whose job is to now to call the meetings, to chair the meetings? We don't know, so nobody does it.

Petitions were made for their replacements, by the way, but it seems like Mystic Springs is stuck in some strange limbo. Jefferson County across to our East insist we fall under the jurisdiction of Rydell Grove, to our West. And let's just say that Rydell Grove don't answer the phone when we ring.

So, we're stuck like this. And we've been managing fine, really.

There was never much crime here anyway, but now the townsfolk know there's no police, they've effectively become the police. Everyone knows everything about everything here. If I leave my house after dark, someone's going to ask me where I'm going. And if I miss my morning walk, I might open the front door later to find a get well card on my porch.

The line begins to shuffle forward and I adopt the same wiggle as the people in front of me.

The sun is setting over the mountains, casting the sky in a warm salmon shade. It would be a nice evening to sit out on my veranda and read a book, try to ignore any passersby, living or spirit.

Slowly, we all file inside. The Hall is set out with chairs in neat rows, that stop being neat as soon as people walk in. Someone needs more room, someone wishes they were on a different row, someone is saving four chairs for people who absolutely will be here, don't you worry. I take a seat next to Nettie Frasier, who gives me a small smile. She's dressed in a navy trouser suit with a huge red flower in her hair, lips crimson as always. I look down at my sandals and tye-dye dress and wonder if I should have dressed up.

I return her smile and then turn my attention to the front of the room.

The last few stragglers find whatever seats are left, and then the door is closed.

To my surprise, Desiree Montag stands up from the front row and walks across to the podium. As the principal of the high school, she must certainly be used to giving speeches, but she's never appeared to relish the opportunity.

She clears her throat.

"Good evening." She begins. Her tone is clear and calm, her speech slow and steady. She's a natural leader, even if she doesn't seem to realise that. "Ladies and gentlemen, thank you for coming out here tonight. As you know, our community has suffered a terrible loss. A person, a child really, a young person with their whole life ahead of them, has had that future taken from them. I believe that many of us in this room didn't get the opportunity to know Lola Anti well enough. I know I didn't."

Whispers circulate around the room. I hear someone mention Desmond's name, then give a laugh. Nettie remains poised by my side.

"Mystic Springs was founded in 1936, when a group of female travellers came across this empty land and set up home. They sent word for their families to join them, and join them they did." Desiree says. She pauses to take a sip of water. "Thanks to our short history as a town, we know more about our roots than most other places do. We know that, until April 1st, this town had never witnessed a murder. I know we all feel heavily the fact that that is no longer true, and that it has changed on our watch."

I swallow. A woman sitting behind me cries softly.

"I also know that Mystic Springs will recover from this." Desiree says. "I know that we are a town of good and kind people, and we will rebuild."

"We're not all good and kind!" An anonymous male voice calls from the crowd, followed by several people telling him to be quiet.

"It's okay." Desiree says. "We do need to stay safe. We're proposing a curfew. Nobody should be out after dark."

The teenagers in the audience all groan at this.

"I hold no power in this town." Desiree admits. "I can stick some of you in detention, but I can't pass a law to say we should all be indoors after dark, or anything else. I'm speaking to you as a friend and suggesting what I think will help us. I think the best way we can get through this troubling time together is to look after one another. Look out for each other, even more than we already do."

"Are the police coming out?" Someone calls from the crowd. I shake my head at their question. Of course the police are coming out.

Desiree lets out a small cough and appears to search through the crowd, looking for a face to reassure her. She smiles suddenly, her face transformed into happiness, as she reaches the eyes of whoever she was searching for. Her son, perhaps.

"We have placed calls with the police department over in Jefferson County and Rydell Grove." Desiree says. She pauses.

"And?" A voice calls.

"At this time, unfortunately, they have no resources to send to us." Desiree says.

Silence falls across the room as her words sink in.

Help is not coming.

Save yourselves.

"Do they know a murder happened?" A vaguely familiar voice calls out.

"They know all of the facts that we have available to us." Desiree says, choosing her words carefully now. "They will send us help, they say, if they can."

"If?"

"If they can." Desiree repeats. "I know that this is troubling, and this is why we all need to be vigilant."

"I'm getting outta here." One man calls, and then there's a commotion as he scoops up an armful of small children, who descend into giggles, and carries them out of the Hall.

"If you want to leave, you can." Desiree says to the remaining crowd. "Nobody will blame you for taking whatever steps you think are needed to protect your family."

A muttering runs through the Hall and several other people stand and leave, casting last glances back towards Desiree as if they're sneaking out of assembly and scared of being caught.

I shift uncomfortably in my seat. I could leave, I guess, but where would I go?

The only relatives I have, apart from Sage, are in England, and I've left it far too long without contact to suddenly arrive on their doorsteps.

I take a deep breath and am reminded yet again why the one time I held my heart out to a man was foolish. Not only did he smash it, stomp on it, cut it into pieces, but I was silly enough to move across the world for him, and he left me with nothing and nobody.

No, I've worked too hard to build a life here for myself. Friends. Work. A life I genuinely love.

I'm not running anywhere.

I rise to my feet slowly, not sure what is coming over me. I fix my gaze on Desiree's and clear my throat.

"I'm staying." I call.

"I'm staying." I repeat, louder. Heads begin to turn towards me, faces break out into smiles.

The Hall becomes deafening with the sound of chairs being pushed back on the uneven wood floor, as people rise to their feet, mimic my actions.

"I'm staying." They chant in chorus, eyes focused on Desiree, who bites her lip and nods slowly.

"I'm staying." The spirits say, filling the centre aisle. I catch Sage's eye and she winks at me.

"I'm staying." Nettie says, rising to perfect posture by my side. I glance towards her but her focus is on the front of the room.

"I'm staying too." Desiree says, and the room erupts with a whoop of crazed delight. We have no reason to sound happy or to appear united. A murderer stands amongst us. And yet, if we do not cling together, we will fall apart.

Violet Warren marches through the crowd and stands next to Desiree at the podium.

"This is our town!" She calls, her voice warbled with age. She raises her arm in the air, loose folds of skin hanging from her skinny arm, makes a fist. "This is Mystic Springs! And we will not be beaten!"

The audience gives her a round of applause.

A young woman with long, strawberry-blond hair, moves through the crowd with the grace of a dancer, all long limbs and light footsteps. She is Eleanor Bean, owner of Screamin' Beans Coffee House, the best place in a 100 mile radius to chill out on a comfortable sofa with a caffeinated slurp of heaven.

"Hello." She says, timid. "I'm Ellie, from the coffee house. If anyone doesn't want to be alone, like me..."

She ignores a whooping from the audience, a cry of 'call me, baby'

"Well, the coffee house will be staying open. And everyone's welcome."

The crowd clap, and Desiree raises a hand towards the audience to take control again. Violet and Ellie return to their seats, but nobody sits back down.

"This is the spirit of Mystic Springs that we all know and love. Everyone needs to stay safe. Look out for each other. But life will continue. And yes, that means school stays open."

A groan works its way around the room, and I spot Mariam Hornblower, the PE teacher, laugh.

"Meeting over." Desiree says, and with a swift businesslike nod, she leaves the podium and disappears into the audience.

I turn to Nettie, who feels my gaze on her and looks towards me. She smiles.

"You were brave, starting all that." She says with a smile.

"Starting all... wow, I guess I did, didn't I?" I ask. My stomach flips as I consider the danger my enthusiasm may have put people in. Had my emotional outburst, my loyalty to this town that owed me nothing but treated me like one of theirs, convinced other people to stay? It must have done.

Nettie shrugs. "It's a little ironic that she suggested a curfew."

"Why?" I ask.

"Because it's dark out now." Nettie says.

"Shall we walk back together?" I ask. The sun was fading when we arrived for the meeting, and as we all filed out of the building, the town was lit by lampposts. The day had ended.

Nettie shook her head. "I drove."

"Oh." I say. She doesn't offer me a lift. "Well, goodnight."

"Yes, goodnight." She says, and we part ways as she walks across the car park. She climbs into a huge 4x4, the newest model, and not the car I saw her drive last week when we passed at traffic lights. I watch her speed out of the lot towards her home.

"I'll walk with you." Mariam says, appearing by my side.

She's the closest I have to a living best friend here, although she's much younger than me, and the reason I would think of calling her that is down to how often she comes for appointments. Every month. Atticus insists on it.

"That was a good meeting, don't you think? Desiree's very calming."

"Oh, she's excellent." Mariam says. She looks good. Her skin is clear, her eyes bright. She's been sober for three years now. "I think she feels guilty too."

"Why?"

"She tried to get Lola to attend school and it ended up in a huge argument. You know what Des is like, wants to save everyone."

"I've been guilty of that in my time. It never works." I say.

6

CONNIE

*A*tticus is here.

I know that much, and I know I'm not talking to him.

My head feels like the town's rock band has taken it up as their new rehearsal space, and despite popping a couple of pills as soon as I got back in from the Town Hall meeting, it's not clearing.

I considered taking a long, hot bath but the thought of being in the bath alone at night while a killer is loose in the town didn't sit too well with me, and so I'm in my living room, drapes closed, doors locked, pretending I haven't noticed Atticus sitting behind me at the dining table.

I still feel buzzed from the meeting, but as the adrenaline settles down, I'm in disbelief that I stood up and announced I would be staying put. And I'm horrified that my actions convinced other people to stay. People I've grown to know and care about over the years. People who've come to me for appointments, cried on my sofa, got the closure they've craved for years.

I feel sick.

"The meeting went well." Atticus says finally, breaking the silence.

I nod but don't turn to him. I don't need to, he floats across the room and sits down in the chair opposite me. He looks old, I realise suddenly, and since spirits can't age, it must be the worry that I see etched into his transparent face.

"You're troubled."

"It's a troubling time." I say. "And you don't look too care-free either."

"I'm not." He admits. "I've devoted my whole life to this town. My father was mayor before me, so even my child-hood was spent wondering how we could make this place better, happier... we never had to worry about it being safer."

"I can't believe they won't send any police." I admit. My stomach flips as I say the words out loud. It feels as if we're stuck in a low budget horror film, the town isolated from help, invaded by a killer. I don't watch horror films, but I'm pretty sure those ones never turn out too well. I should have ran out of the Town Hall and found the first plane to England.

Atticus shrugs. "It's the hand we've been dealt. We can fight it or we can solve the case ourselves."

I groan. "Has Sage sent you?"

Where is Sage?

"No, but I know she's spoken to you. You know about the Sheriff's investigation."

"I can't help." I say, and I stand up and walk across to the kitchen, bare feet on linoleum floor. I take a bottle of white wine from the fridge and add a small drop to a glass, then top it up with lemonade. I'm really a pathetic drinker, and I don't want a hangover in the morning.

When I return to the living room, Sage is pacing the room. She greets me with a nervous smile.

"I have my first suspect." She says.

"You - what? Already?" I stammer.

Sage nods and her pacing picks up speed. I take a greedy sip of my drink and remain standing, feeling myself being pulled in to something I don't want to be involved in. It feels the way my teenage years did, when all I wanted to focus on was cute boys and learning how to straighten my hair (I gave up on both, the hair straightening before the boys), and instead I was visited too frequently by spirits.

I was never scared when they showed up, in my bedroom usually, but whenever they weren't there, I was terrified of the thought of them. Spirits, in my mind, were scary, unnatural and ominous. It took a while for me to realise that in truth, they're just as they were as people, usually a little dopey, easily confused and more concerned about themselves than wanting bad for other people.

A full year after my dead headmaster visited me, I realised that this gift - or curse - wasn't going anywhere, and I started trying to enjoy it. But I kept it secret, knowing that anyone I told wouldn't believe me.

"Who is it?" Atticus asks, rubbing his white stubble thoughtfully.

"Desiree." Sage says.

"What?!" I ask. "Desiree? Are you insane?"

"Erm..." Sage stumbles over her words. "She argued with Lola. It needs checking out."

"Hold on." I say, thinking back to Mariam's words earlier that evening. "Were you listening to me talk to Mariam?"

"Mariam's not involved." Atticus says, fiercely protective of his daughter.

"I was just flitting around, I was listening to everyone.

That's my job, remember, in the Sheriff's investigation." Sage says, and she sticks her chest out a little with pride.

"An argument isn't enough to make someone a suspect." I say, then wonder where I am getting my confidence from. "Is it?"

"If it's all we have to go on, we need to follow it as a lead." Atticus says with a decisive nod.

That's hard to argue with, I have to admit, but I just want to slurp my lemonade-wine and then crash into my soft bed for a deep sleep. I do not want to talk about murder before bed. That's not unreasonable, is it?

"Guys, I'm going to leave ya'll to it." I say, and leave the room. There must be something unusually firm in my tone of voice because they don't follow me. I get into my pyjamas and climb into bed, pulling the comforter over me. I set the wine on the bedside table and fall into a deep sleep with the muffled voices of the ghosts in my living room as the sound-track in the background.

**

"Ugh!" I say as the bitter taste hits me. I've taken a swig of the lemonade-wine, forgetting that it's not my normal glass of water - that'll teach me for not using wine glasses. I dart across to the en suite and brush my teeth, scrubbing my tongue particularly hard, and then return to bed, where I sit up and listen to the silence of the empty house.

I've always enjoyed silence, which surprises people because I'm bubbly in that way that overweight people feel they need to be to compensate for the fact we're not a size zero. I don't think I was a size zero when I was born. Baby photos reveal rolls of fat, puppy fat I never grew out of. While the boys at school were practically drooling over Sage, with her glossy hair and slim figure, I made them laugh with my personality. I learnt to crack crude jokes and how to perfectly time a punch line, and later I learnt how to change the oil in my car and check myself into a flight for a solo holiday, while Sage learnt how to make men fall in love with her and rescue her whenever she needed help.

My independence might have been forced on me by the fact that no boys were throwing themselves at my feet like they were at Sage's, but I grew to love it. I realised I could do everything, pretty much, for myself.

And as we got older, I saw my confidence grow, while Sage lost her spark. Tied down with a husband, a house and two little mouths to feed, her sense of magic and excitement left her. Bill by bill, laundry load by laundry load, she realised that life wasn't the grand adventure it had pretended to be. Me? I'd always expected life to be work, and not fair (try being a teenage girl with raging hormones that make you fancy every boy you see, when their only interest in you is to ask for your sister's phone number). And I was right.

My phone rings, and I jump a little at the incessant high-pitched tune.

I don't know about you, but my phone actually being used for a phone call is something of a rarity these days.

I glance at the screen, unknown number.

Against my better judgement, I answer. "Hello?"

"Is that Connie Winters?" The male voice is too upbeat, too happy. It must be a sales call.

"Yes..." I admit warily.

"I'm calling from the Jefferson County Tribune, do you have a few moments?"

"I guess, what's this about? How did you get my number?"

"Oh, a friend of yours gave it to us, said you'd want to take this call!"

"A friend?" I repeat. I'm pretty sure none of my real friends would hand out my phone number to a newspaper I don't read.

"Uh-huh, that's right ma'am." He says, and I can picture the false smile plastered across his face to help him keep his tone light and fantastic.

"Are you a reporter or is this about advertising space?" I ask. Every year or so I get calls from the Tribune asking me to buy space in their newspaper, and on the free wall calendar they produce for readers. I never buy.

"Oh, I'm Anish Shah, you've probably heard of me." He says.

"I don't think so." I admit.

He laughs. "Damn lady, you're a tough cookie! You could at least pretend like everyone else does."

I find myself returning his laugh, happy to have got him to go off-script.

"So, Anish-Shah-I've-never-heard-of, how can I help?"

"We're doing a story on the terrible murder and how dangerous Mystic Springs is, and I wanted to try and get a quote from Lola."

"Lola?" I say, my stomach churning.

"Mm-hmm, yes ma'am, it would be a great exclusive for us. The Tribune is the oldest independent newspaper in the state, you know, and any support for us is..."

"Lola's dead." I say bluntly. I'm annoyed that he hasn't done his research before calling. Journalists are so lazy nowadays.

"I know, ma'am, that's why I'm ringing you."

My stomach flips as I realise what he means. He wants a quote from a ghost for his article. I realise how he got my number; anyone could have passed my number on if he rang them, played ignorant, asked for the medium's number. I sigh.

"It doesn't work that way." I say.

"Okay, sure." He lets out a nervous laugh. "I'm kinda new to the whole ghost thing, so you can educate me, how does it work?"

"The spirits decide if they want to be contacted. They can say no to any request just like I can refuse to answer my door to a guest - or my phone to a caller." I explain. I can recite these things without thinking about them. I warn all new clients of this, to try and control the disappointment they will feel if the person they're trying to contact refuses them.

"So how do I file a request to contact Lola?" Anish asks. I can't quite work out if his tone is sincere, and visions of his newspaper running a report on me as a kooky medium flash before my mind. I don't read that paper, but still.

"Well, I see clients. I have a waiting list, though." I say. I'm damn good at what I do and word has spread. I don't need to advertise, that's why I never buy the space in his paper.

"I'll pay double if you can fit me in today." He says.

"That's impossible." I say.

"I'll pay three times. And, listen, I like you ma'am, but you gotta understand that this story will run, with or without you. I heard some interesting things about how you're telling people to stay in town. Are your ghost friends telling you that's a good idea?"

My body tenses.

"I don't appreciate the threat. You'll be running this story without me." I say, and end the call.

I shake my head and dive back under the covers, switching my phone on to silent so nobody else can disturb me from the rare day of rest I have planned.

7

SAGE

*I*t's tomorrow, and I'm the first one in the attic, without Connie.

I know Patton Davey told me not to bother returning without her, but I've got good information. Two suspects! He'll hear my ideas and have no choice but to keep me on the investigating team. I hope.

Don't get me wrong, this isn't my life calling or anything, but being a spirit can be a little dull. Just like life, I guess. A murder investigation would keep me busy. And it sounds exciting! I mean, it's not like the murderer can kill me if I mess up, is it? Ha!

I sense another presence in the dusty old room and look up to see Patton float in. He's so handsome, damn it. Handsome and intimidating. I've always loved that combination. Well, handsome and anything really.

"Sage." He greets, then carefully lowers himself onto a chair. He looks tired.

"Good morning Sheriff." I say in my best lilting sing-song voice.

"No Connie?" He asks, an eyebrow raised.

"It's early yet." I say, although I know she isn't coming. I haven't even told her about the meeting, or the fact that a few of us are hiding out in her attic. "I'm early. I have a couple of leads to tell you about."

"Already?" He asks.

I nod. "I got to work straightaway."

"That's impressive." He says. Patton Davey was a fair man and he's a fair spirit and I knew, well I hoped, that if I had solid information, he'd rethink his decision that I'm only valuable if my sister's involved. "Is there a reason you don't want to say with Atticus here?"

My cheeks flush as I realise he must wonder if Atticus is one of my suspects. "Oh, my, no! No! Nothing like that... I was just keen to see you. To share the information, I mean."

Stop talking, Sage.

"I'd rather share the information freely amongst the group, so let's wait for Atticus to make an appearance. He's never usually late." Patton says, remaining poised and professional as my cheeks burn crimson.

"Of course. You're the sheriff, Sheriff."

Seriously. Tape up your mouth and BE QUIET!

I begin to fiddle with my long necklace, twirling each bead in turn to keep me occupied - and silent.

The door opens after a few minutes, and in walks Atticus, followed by Connie.

Still in her pyjamas, she looks pale and nervous. A huge mug of coffee is clasped in her hands. She searches the room for me and shoots me a look that means I'm in trouble later, but she still sits next to me so it can't be too bad.

"Thanks for coming." I whisper.

"Don't." She shoots back without making eye contact.

Patton clears his throat. "Ok, thank you all. We'll start with questions."

I look across from Patton towards Atticus, and then to Connie. Nobody raises their hands or makes any indication that they want to begin.

"No questions? Let me give an overview then." Patton says. "We'll form a task force to investigate the murder of Lola Anti. This attic will be HQ and we'll meet daily. Speed is everything with a murder investigation. Evidence is, literally, disappearing by the hour. The murder weapon, for example, was still with the victim when she was discovered but it's location now is unknown."

"The knife's gone missing?" I ask.

Patton nods. "The best guess here is that the killer returned to the scene to retrieve it, but we have to be careful of guesses and assumptions. This is an investigation, we gather facts and evidence."

Atticus nods slowly. "We can search for the knife?"

"We can, sir, that's right. We do have a photograph of it. For once, people's obsession with their smartphones has worked in our favour."

I gulped. "Do you mean...?"

"Someone at the party took a photograph of Lola's body, yes ma'am."

"Wow." I whispered.

"Now, I know we have some leads already, so I'd like to hand over to Sage to share what she has."

I shift in my seat. I didn't expect to be sharing my information. I thought I'd report to Patton, he'd filter the valuable information from the irrelevant, and share it with the group in his authoritative, adorable voice while I sat and gazed at him a little too longingly.

"Erm, so... I don't know if this is useful or not. But I've found out about two arguments Lola had before she died."

"That sounds like valuable information." Patton says.

"Thank you. The first person is Nettie Frasier. Everyone knows that her husband had an affair with Lola before his death. I actually witnessed Lola arguing with Nettie before she died. Nettie slapped her, pretty hard, around the face."

"Goodness." Atticus says with a sharp intake of breath.

"And the second person is Desiree Montag. She apparently had an argument with Lola about her not enrolling in school. I don't know much about that one."

"This is good information, Sage, well done." Patton says.

I grin, despite myself.

"Connie, thank you for joining us." Patton says then. "Has Sage told you about how we see your role here?"

Connie still won't meet my eye. "Yes, she told me a little. I'm not happy about being here, but I can't see that you have another choice. And the town needs us."

"It absolutely does, ma'am." Patton says.

"The town needs us to solve this case, it's awful for our reputation. We'll see tourism decline. Economically it's a disaster and it gets worse every day it goes on." Atticus says as he pushes his narrow glasses up his nose.

Connie sighs next to me. "What do you want me to do?"

"Nothing yet." Patton says. "The funeral will be in a couple of days. We need to be able to watch people's behaviour there, and then we'll strike. Until then, keep watching, listening, and gathering information. We'll meet back here tomorrow."

"Okay." Connie says. She makes no attempt to move, and I sit next to her until Atticus and Patton have both floated away.

"Thank you." I whisper again, when it's just the two of us.

"Are you kidding me?" Connie asks with a shake of her head. "Using my attic without even asking?"

I swallow. I knew this was coming. "I'm sorry. Nobody felt comfortable staying in the Baker house."

"This is my home, Sage. I have a right to know who's here. Don't pull a stunt like this again."

"I won't. I'm sorry." I say. I have plenty of tools to get my way with Connie, but when she catches me doing wrong, a sincere apology is the best way to disarm her.

She turns to me then and flashes a weak smile. Forgiven already. "This is insane."

"Your whole life is insane. You're sitting with your dead sister."

Connie laughs and the tension eases. She lets out a deep breath.

"Here's something else that's insane." I say.

Connie looks nervous.

"Patton Davey thought that Atticus was one of my suspects." I say with a laugh.

Connie's eyes widen. "What? That doesn't even make sense."

"I know." I say. "He obviously wasn't thinking straight."

Connie shakes her head and we sit together in silence for a few moments. Connie's lost in her thoughts, and I'm replaying the moment when Patton flattered me for my excellent work. I could get used to being complimented by him. I'm lost in a daydream of me solving the case and Patton declaring his undying love and admiration for me when Connie interrupts me.

"Sage? Are you listening?"

"Erm, no." I admit. "I was miles away, sorry."

"I said... what if a spirit should be a suspect?" Connie says.

Her words make me laugh. Everyone knows that spirits can't interfere with the human realm. Sure, we can hang around in human places, and some humans can see us and communicate with us. And, yes, there are bad spirits, the ones who have a grudge against someone still, but really all they can do is scare people. A new spirit can't even touch physical objects and plenty of spirits never learn the skill; it's hard work and draining. Like any muscle, your ghostly connection to real world objects needs to be stretched with consistent practice.

But a spirit hurting, never mind killing, a person? Unheard of.

"You really are insane." I say with an eye roll.

Connie nods and jumps up to her feet. "You're right. I'm going to grab a coffee, fancy coming?"

"Sure." I say.

We leave the house and stroll across town together to The Promenade, the shopping complex where the coffee house is, each lost in our thoughts. Despite Connie's reservations, she'll be great helping me out on the investigation. I've already proven myself to be the key member of the team, so really all she will have to do is take a confession from the killer when I find them. I wonder if Patton will make me his deputy. That would be a hoot.

Screamin' Beans is an adorable coffee house. Of course, it opened long after I passed, so I've never got to taste the drinks that everyone raves about, but it has a great vibe. Lots of spirits hang out here, especially towards closing time when it's getting more empty. We take an old battered leather settee near the window, where we can people watch.

We have company. Ellie's enormous Persian cat, Godiva, spends all of her time strolling around the coffee house and looking at each visitor in disgust. She can see me, I'm fairly sure, judging by the way she squints her eyes and glares in my direction as normal.

"That cat must be bad for business." I grumble.

"Oh come on, she's adorable." Connie says.

"No way, she's scary. And what about allergies?"

Connie laughs. "You don't have allergies."

"Well no but that's me all over, fighting for the voiceless, standing up for those in need..."

"You're funny." Connie says. "Hey, don't let this investigation change you. Stay grounded."

"Oh shut up." I retort, hearing the sarcasm in her voice.

The people of Mystic Springs know Connie well enough that they don't give her a second glance when she talks in public to a spirit they can't see. The believers like to see her doing homework, and the non-believers treat her with the understanding all crazy people deserve.

Violet Warren bursts in the door then in neon pink lycra leggings and a fitted sports tank top. She searches the coffee house, finds Connie, and dashes across.

"Connie!" She calls across the room.

"Oh God." Connie says, sinking in her side of the settee a little.

"I thought I saw you in the window, I need some help." She says, dropping down into the leather chair closest to my side of the settee, as if she senses my presence, which she absolutely doesn't. Violet is entirely focused on the human realm.

"Sure, what's up?"

"I need a meeting."

"Oh, ok. Sure, we can get something planned."

"Today." Violet says.

I roll my eyes. Everyone and their damn dog needs an appointment today.

"I can't do today."

"You have to." Violet says, leaning in close. Her lipstick is hot pink and a little wonky, and the sight makes me feel ridiculously sad for her for some reason.

"You can fit her in." I whisper, although there's no need for me to lower my voice. It's habit. Spirits speak at a pitch that most living people can't hear. "She might know something about the case."

Connie glances at me and frowns, then nods.

"Well, if it's urgent, I could see you later I guess. Give me two hours, okay?"

Violet nods and looks at her watch. "That's perfect, I'm off to hot yoga now. I'll be sweaty when I see you next!"

"I can hardly wait." Connie mutters as Violet leaps up and dashes out of the coffee house, heading for the nearby gym.

8

SAGE

*V*iolet's late, which considering the urgent need for the meeting, is pretty hilarious.

I wouldn't say that to Connie, though.

She's given the sitting room that she uses to see clients a good polish and tidy, to clear the energy for any spirits to come through, and is now just pacing. She always gets like this before appointments. I consider telling her to relax but decide against it.

"I was thinking, I should stick around." I say. I'm in the kitchen, because she bans me from the consultation room before and during appointments in case my energy pollutes the process.

"No way." Connie says. She pours two glasses of water and carries them in to the room.

"I need to gather as much info as I can." I say. "And I'm pretty sure you can keep me separate from whoever she wants to see. You know my energy well enough, I've been haunting you for twenty years remember."

Connie rolls her eyes. "Don't say that word."

"Woooooooooo!" I say in my best ghost impression.

"Cut it out." Connie says. "All that silly ghost talk is the reason why my industry is so disrespected."

"Oh, lighten up." I whine.

She glares at me and then the doorbell rings. I try one last effort, the old eyelash flutter, and a bit of emotional pressure. "You know, maybe twenty years is long enough. Maybe I'm not wanted here anymore."

"Oh fine." Connie snaps as she goes to answer the door. "But sit in the corner and don't make any noise at all."

"Yes, boss!" I sing out and float across to the room. It's a cute room, designed to be reassuring for all of the nervous people who come in here. It's very light and airy, to get rid of any fear people might have about ghosts being dark and scary, and there are two identical settees facing each other, with a coffee table in between. A decorative box of tissues sits on the table, and Connie has already set out the water for each of them. Other than that, the room is pretty bare. It could be the setting for some high-end therapy. Actually, I guess it kind of is, in a way. You wouldn't believe some of the problems people bring in with them. It's never used for anything but meetings, and Connie wants to keep the energy in the room focused, so there are no distractions. No pictures on the walls, no bookcase, definitely no TV.

Violet bursts in and takes a seat. If she has a spirit animal, it's the Tasmanian devil.

In her hand, she holds a fabric headband covered in a pale pink floral design.

"This was hers." She says, handing it across to Connie, who refuses to take it.

"Let me explain the process." Connie says.

Violet rolls her eyes.

"I have to do it." Connie says. She's such a role follower. I stifle a giggle as she begins to give the guidelines she knows by memory. "You're here to ask me to make contact with a spirit. You've brought an item that belonged to the person, I'll take that from you shortly, and that will help me connect with them. I also ask that you keep the person at the front of your thoughts throughout. Please drink plenty of water during this meeting. No tea, coffee, alcohol, etc is allowed. Just water. We keep the energy clean in this room. There is no guarantee that I will be able to contact the person you wish me to. I cannot simply summon a spirit. Spirits choose whether they respond to my attempts to contact them, and there can be many reasons why a spirit would not respond. In particular, spirits who have crossed over recently will still be learning how to move around as a spirit and tune in to my contact. My fee is non-refundable. Does that all make sense?"

Violet nods. "Yes, yes, let's get on with it."

She holds the headband across to Connie again, and she takes it this time.

She clasps the material in her hands and closes her eyes. Violet sits on her hands.

"You want to speak to Lola." Connie says after a few moments, opening her eyes.

"Yes I do." Violet says.

"Do you have a question for her?"

Violet nods.

"You can ask it out loud. Think of her as you say it."

"I want to know where my purple shoes are." Violet says, and I have to float out of the room for a second to compose myself. I force myself to think about the time when I was a teenager and my brand new hairdryer blew up, leaving me stuck with wet and wild hair right before a date. That takes the smile off my face and I float right back in.

"Lola, if you can hear us, Violet is here and she'd like to

connect with you." Connie says. She's used to hearing ridiculous things said between the living and the spirits. The things that people think are important enough to need to say to a dead person are insane. Once, she had a widow who came on every anniversary of her husband's death to remind him she hadn't forgiven him for dying. The husband turned up every year, still dressed in his chef's hat, hoping for her to declare her love for him, and then skulked away again. In the end, Connie decided the whole thing was too cruel and stopped answering the woman's calls. She died herself not that long ago and I can tell you she's making that poor man's afterlife Hell.

"Well? Is she coming?" Violet asks.

"It can take time." Connie says. "Why don't you share a few memories of Lola, that will help her sense our energy."

Violet snorts at the suggestion. "I remember her moving my purple shoes and not telling me where she'd put them! And I remember her being late every single day. That's the problem with the young, you say start at nine and they think that means ten past."

"What were the things you liked most about her?" Connie asks. It's amazing how she remains professional.

Violet takes a deep breath and considers the question. She's either treating it very seriously, or she didn't like the dead girl much at all.

"She reminded me of myself I guess, when I was younger." Violet says after an age.

Connie smiles. "How so?"

"Well, she was independent, and I've always been alone. No husband or kids. Just me, and I've been fine. Lola was like that, wasn't she, running away and ending up here."

"What made you hire her?" Connie asks. Lola had been Violet's carer, although nobody had understood why this woman who flitted from hot yoga to naked swimming in the springs needed a carer.

"She seemed fun and headstrong. And she needed help. She couldn't rely on that dreadful man for money, I wasn't going to watch that happen." Violet says with a shrug. "Is she here yet? I really do need to find my shoes."

"Lola, we're talking about the good memories we have of you. If you can hear me, we invite you to come and join us." Connie says. She closes her eyes when she speaks to a spirit in these meetings, but that's for effect. Clients have usually been to see a few charlatan mediums, or watched the dramatic mediums on TV, and they can feel underwhelmed with Connie's work as a professional, ethical medium. There's no sudden possessions of her body, no speaking in tongues, just a nice, calm meeting. You can tell she's British.

"Tell her it's not funny." Violet says, crossing her arms over her sagging bosom.

"She can hear you." Connie says. "The spirits have no issue hearing us, it's just that most people can't hear or see them. You can just talk and she'll be able to hear. But like I said, she's only recently crossed over, she might not know how to respond yet."

"Well." Violet says. "If it's just me talking out loud I could have stayed at home for that."

"Yes you could." Connie says. "But you know I can't ever guarantee a response."

"Oh, I know." Violet says. And she's fine for the money, trust me. She made a fortune doing some crazy type of art, huge pictures as colourful as her wardrobe. She can spend a few dollars on a consultation. "Is it harder? For a person who was murdered?"

I can feel Connie's discomfort. "Yes. It can be. We don't talk about how a person died, unless they raise it."

"Will she be happy now, though? She wasn't very happy when she was alive."

"She wasn't?" Connie asks. My ears prick up with attention.

"She hated everything. She hated work, she hated me. If we had any police, they'd be taking me in for questioning."

"Why would you say that?"

"Well, I'm the prime suspect."

"Are you?"

"Of course I am. She was slacking at work, really taking advantage of my good nature."

"By arriving a bit late?"

"Huh!" Violet exclaimed. "That's just the start. She'd take lunch breaks that lasted three hours, arrive back to work with a fresh hickey on her neck. Just before she died, we had a screaming row about her attitude. I was pretty hard on her."

"I didn't know any of that." Connie says.

"Well, you wouldn't. I pushed that girl, I wanted her to realise she could do more than just be a rich man's play-thing. Where's the motivation to work hard though, when your rent's being paid, when you can have anything you want from your sugar daddy."

I take a deep breath inwards. I'd be pretty happy with that deal, I think.

"She's not coming, is she?" Violet says.

"No." Connie admits. "I don't think she is. It might just be too soon, Violet. You could come back in a month if you wanted."

"Puh, forget it. If I don't find my shoes this week I'll have to replace them."

"Are you just here about the shoes? Nothing else you wanted to say?"

"What else would I say to her?" Violet asks, incredulous. "I've already told you, we didn't particularly like each other."

"Okay. Well, I'm sorry." Connie says.

Violet bends down and roots around in her handbag, then hands Connie a handful of notes.

"I'll see you around." Violet says. "Thanks for trying."

Connie walks her to the door and while she does, I close the consultation room door and take a seat back in the kitchen. Connie doesn't return into the house, though, and after a few minutes I follow her trail and find her on one of the rocking chairs on the veranda.

"You ok?" I ask.

She nods. "I can't believe the only person who has tried to see Lola did it because of some damn shoes."

I laugh.

"I'm serious, Sage. You'd hope you'd be more missed than that, surely?"

I ponder the question. "I guess so."

"Oh come on, imagine if all I'd wanted from you was something like that."

"I get your point." I say. "But, the fact is, Lola doesn't seem to have a lot of friends in this town, and who knows what she was running from before she came here. I don't know that we should be blaming people for not losing sleep over someone they didn't like that much."

Connie sighs. "She was just a kid."

"Exactly. That makes it even more tragic, but people shouldn't suddenly pretend she was their favourite person."

"Ah, you're right." Connie says. "This is why I can't do too many of these appointments, it's so draining."

"Listen to your wise sister." I say. I've been telling her for months to put a limit on her meetings.

"I know, I know." Connie says. She pulls a blanket from

the wooden box kept on the veranda solely to store spare cushions and blankets, and wraps herself in it, then closes her eyes.

I know sometimes she wishes she didn't have this gift. I see the pain and tiredness it causes her sometimes. But I'm so pleased she does have it. Or I wouldn't be able to have moments like this. Moments of noticing that she's pulled the blanket across at a bad angle, so one of her feet isn't tucked in. I reach across and straighten the blanket, covering her foot.

"I love you." She murmurs as she drifts off to sleep.

Maybe I'm a bad person, but I'll let her have the tiredness if it buys me more moments like this.

9

CONNIE

*B*RITISH GHOST HUNTER TELLS LOCALS TO STICK AROUND... WITH MURDERER!

"Are you kidding me?" I ask as Ellie Bean slides the newspaper across the counter to me while she prepares my cappuccino. "I knew that reporter was bad news. Why has he mentioned I'm British? How is that relevant?"

"You're an outsider." Ellie says with a shrug. She must see the horror on my face because her pale face reddens. "Oh no, no, I didn't mean it like that. We don't think of you like that. But you weren't born here. He's going for the 'us and them' angle, isn't he?"

"I guess." I say. I slide the newspaper back across towards her. "I can't believe that's the main story, not the murder itself. Or the lack of police help."

"Don't let it bother you." Ellie says as she hands me my drink. "We're all on your side."

"I guess. Thanks." I say. I take a seat by the window of the empty coffee shop and allow my thoughts to wander.

Today is Lola's funeral and, for some reason I can't think of, I'm going to attend. I generally don't attend funerals, my thinking being that I see enough of people after they've died as it is. But I'm still feeling shook up by Violet's visit, and the lack of mourning the town is showing. I guess I'm scared nobody will attend, which I realise I wouldn't know about if I didn't attend, but at least by me being there, I can make sure it's not completely ignored.

I've pulled out my oldest clothes from the wardrobe, and I feel completely uncomfortable in my skin. The blazer jacket I'm wearing isn't fitted, it kind of hangs around me, but it's black as night. I've stayed with a bright dress, at least. It's been a long time since my clothes choices were based on anything other than which items are good value, look pretty, and feel comfortable. Geeze, that makes me sound old.

"Have you seen this?"

I glance up. Desiree Montag stands in front of me, the newspaper in her hand. I'd hoped that Ellie might discard it instead of adding it to the rack. "Yep."

"I can't stand reporters. Did they even speak to you?" Desiree takes a seat opposite me. Dressed in her normal business wear, she has a fitted black blouse and black trousers on. Her hair hangs in shoulder-length dreadlocks. She's the epitome of professional, and just sitting by her side makes me feel sloppy.

"Someone rang me." I say. This encounter is strange. Desiree is usually far too busy, or reserved, or shy perhaps, to come and start a conversation. With me, anyway. "Asked me to give him a quote from Lola."

"Ugh." She says. "Those people have no standards. I really hoped Anish would do better."

"You know him?"

"He was a student." Desiree says. She's travelled a lot,

moving from place to place to teach, never staying as long as she's been in Mystic Springs. There were rumours for years that she had something to hide and, if they were true, she's doing a damn good job of it.

"Well, he's only doing his job, I guess."

"That excuse doesn't give people a pass to get out of doing the right thing." Desiree says. "I'm sorry I butted in on your quiet time like this, I know we don't even know each other too well. But I saw the headline. Just wanted to show my support."

"Thank you." I say.

"Ask her about the argument." Sage whispers, making me jump. I didn't even notice her float in.

"It's so sad... about Lola." I say, stumbling for the right words. "Did you know her much?"

Desiree shakes her head sadly. "I wasn't her favourite person."

"You're kidding?" I ask, my false surprise a little too obvious. Desiree is lost deep in her memories, though, and doesn't notice.

"She was anti-education." She says after a few moments. "Anti-rules. We clashed a few times."

"Oh, she didn't like you because you represented education?" I say.

"Well, no, it's more than that." Desiree says as she shifts in her seat uncomfortably. "I probably overstepped my mark a little, trying to get her to enrol."

"Yeah." I say. "Seems like she was all about freedom."

"I'd say she was all about manipulation." Desiree says, holding my gaze.

"What do you mean?" I ask. This wasn't the way she had made it sound at the Town Hall meeting.

"She was manipulating Desmond Frasier." Desiree says. "And she manipulated me."

I'm about to ask for more information when I spot the time on the wall clock. If I want to make it to the funeral, I need to set off. Desiree catches the distraction on my face. "Are you going to the funeral?"

I nod.

"Me too. Shall we walk together?" Desiree says to my surprise.

We finish last sips of our drinks and leave the coffee house together, walking in a strained silence until my curiosity can't stand it.

"What happened, with her and you?"

Desiree sighs. "I broke the rules."

Now that was impossible to picture.

"They warn you about it, when you're training. But training isn't like real life, with real kids. She was so messed up when she arrived, I found her sleeping in the gymnasium. Begged her to enrol. She wouldn't hear any of it. I let it go that once, just gave her some cash for food and told her to stay safe. But the next day she was back. I told her the best way I could help her would be getting her enrolled, so she could start getting some options for her life, but she wouldn't hear it. I had to call the police, that's what my training says. She was a runaway, I should have called it in. But she started blackmailing me."

"What?" I ask, her words stopping me in my tracks. I gaze at Desiree, mouth open.

She nods. "I'd been paying her for a year before she was killed."

I can hear the music from the church up ahead. We're late. I increase the pace of my walking, even as my mind reels from her confession.

"But." I begin. "I don't get it. What could she possibly have as ammunition to blackmail you with?"

My words are lost in the noise as we enter the church. I've never seen such a crowded service. The whole town, apparently, are here. Several Mystic Springs High students are here, in uniform, and several spirits are gathered around the edges of the room. Spirits love funerals. They rarely get to see their own, because of the issues with appearing so quickly after their own death, and so they jump at the chance to see other services.

Desiree catches my eye and flashes me a tight smile, but as I turn into a row at the back of the space, she strides down the nave and stands next to the group of students who are, I realise, the choir.

I stand, shellshocked, while people around me talk and cough.

I spot Violet Warren a few rows ahead of me, her outfit making no concessions for the sombre occasion.

"I know I'm the prime suspect." She announces, to anyone who wants to listen, it seems. "Anyone want a sweet?"

She hands out a paper bag of boiled sweets. In my shock, I take one - pineapple - and by the time we're asked to rise and sing the first hymn, several of us have to mumble as best we can with our mouths full of the damn things.

"And now we'll hear Lola's favourite song, performed by the Mystic Springs High School choir." The vicar announces, his voice low and thick with remorse, even though I can't imagine when his path has ever crossed with Lola's.

Desiree moves out of the aisle and the choir file past her. She touches the arm of each student as they walk up to the chancel.

For a small town, the quality of the choir is staggering. I haven't heard them perform often, not being a regular church-goer and having no reason to attend the school for events. Some people who are child-free, or with grown up kids, still attend the high school events, so I'd be welcome. But I think that's one Americanism that I haven't picked up. I have no children. I don't get involved with school.

I listen to the beautiful voices of the young men and women, all around Lola's age, and am surprised by how emotional it makes me. The last funeral I attended was Sage's, and I have never been more sad on any day of my life before or since. I'd been living in America for a few years by then, and our contact had dwindled so much that on the one trip she made across to see me with her two daughters, she'd flippantly introduced me as some second cousin. Her words had stung, because she'd been as bad at staying in touch as I had, but I could hardly correct her in front of those two beautiful nieces I barely knew.

The trip had been heartbreaking for me. The plans I'd had, of showing my wild and carefree sister around, quickly fell down around me. I barely knew her any more. She carried life's burdens so visibly, it was as if she were walking with a stoop. Underneath that, though, was the anger. The pure, bitter anger that life had conned her. Her grand adventure hadn't arrived, and she'd given up hope that it was on its way.

They flew back home as planned, and contact between us reduced even further.

She was dead a few months later.

The choir stop singing and I realise I am sobbing. Like, full on, snot-bubbles ugly crying. A few people around me are watching me with interest.

I shake my head and run out of the church, stopping

after a few moments as my body reminds me that I'm no runner. Still sobbing, but now out of breath as well, I slow down and walk across the empty town towards my house. All I want is to climb into my bed and sleep.

A noise from across the street catches my attention, and I turn to see Nettie Frasier, hair pulled into a tight bun, watering the hanging baskets by her front door.

She has plenty of reasons not to mourn Lola, of course, but I'm still shocked to see her so publicly boycotting the funeral. She turns and notices me and for a few seconds we watch each other, then she turns and walks into her home, slamming the door behind her.

"Oh my goodness, what's wrong?" Sage asks, appearing by my side. She hates to see people crying. It distresses her to watch perfectly applied make-up be ruined, or clear skin become puffy.

I continue crying and she floats along beside me, waiting for me to catch my breath.

"I'm so sorry I wasn't a better sister." I finally say.

To my surprise, she laughs. "Geeze! You've been named and shamed by the newspaper, we have a murderer to catch, and you're dragging up things that are 20 years old? You're crazy."

I force myself to laugh. I am crazy.

I've got more than enough to worry about without focusing on the past.

"You're right." I admit. "And... I think you could also be right about Desiree."

Sage grins as if she's just got a free pass out of detention.

"Come on, sis." She says. "Let's solve this case."

10

CONNIE

Mystic Springs is a wealthy town, which makes no sense because until Atticus created the illusion of the springs having magical healing properties, there was no industry to support the town and no determined work ethic among the inhabitants. It's one of those odd things about this place. It seems to have attracted people with independent wealth, and by far the wealthiest is Violet Warren. A respected, perhaps even famed, artist, she rarely mentions her work or her success, but there are parts of the country where, if she went out in public, she would be recognised and mobbed.

Her home is the largest in the town, a sprawling water-front mansion that I've never had cause to enter before.

When I knock, she doesn't seem surprised, and grabs me in a hug. Her bones are all in the right place and I can feel every one of them poking into my flab. I tactically move away an inch, uncomfortable with her feeling the curves of my body in such an intimate way.

"Come in, come in!" She cries, and leads the way

through the whole of the house. I peek into beautiful rooms housing a grand piano, a home gym, a kitchen that looks fresh out of an ideal living magazine, and then finally we walk through the art studio. The huge space has double-height windows along one wall, and the light that pours in and highlights the art pieces strewn across the room is incredible.

I'm not an art fan. I'm pretty clueless and I don't know my oils from my watercolours even, but I see instantly why Violet has the big house.

"These are amazing." I say.

Violet wrinkles her nose up. "They're average."

"Oh, don't be modest. They're incredible."

"No, trust me." Violet says. She pulls the rag from another piece, but I don't know what I'm looking at. While the others were instantly recognisable paintings of people; a man smoking a cigar, a woman crying, a child eating an apple - this one is, clearly, *art*. Vivid lines and shapes, all arranged in a way that I know isn't haphazard, but which looks like it. It's the type of art that I don't understand. "This is the best one I'm working on."

"Wow." I say, because I can't find a more specific response.

"It's okay." Violet says with a laugh. "Everyone prefers those ones. A dear friend asked me to paint for her, and I know she'll love them - it's her family on canvas after all, but they're like everything else out there. It's funny, art's the only industry there is where the more commercial something is, the less it's worth."

"I don't..."

"This one." She says, gesturing to the confusing artpiece. "This will bring in more money. It has more meaning. It's unique. But the other kind are commercial. If you were a working artist, trying to get by month to month, you'd do the commercial stuff and it would pay the bills. But you'd never make real money. You have to be prepared to starve for a while so you can find your real style."

I can't imagine Violet ever starving. In fact, I'd always assumed that she came from money and went into art because she didn't have to pay the bills.

"Come on, let's sit by the water." She says. We walk out of the studio into the mudroom, and out into the lawn. Two wooden chairs sit by the water's edge, and we take one each.

"It's beautiful out here." I say. The river separates Mystic Springs from Rydell Grove, and as I sit in Violet's chair, I can make out small dots of people who must be sitting out in their lawns watching us. I'm tempted to wave, but don't want to look like a tourist.

"So?" Violet says.

"I wanted to pick your brains."

"Ha, good luck with that. Go for it."

"Nettie Frasier."

"Hmm."

"Do you know much about her?"

"Why are you asking?" Violet asks.

"Well, erm..."

"This isn't going to end up in the Tribune, is it?"

My cheeks flush. "No! I didn't speak to the reporter, he rang me and I told him I wouldn't talk. He wanted to get a quote from Lola."

Violet snorts. "Don't we all. I still can't find my purple shoes."

"I'd never speak to a newspaper."

"Okay, I believe you. So, you just want to know, what? General... stuff?"

"I guess." I say. For some reason, I'd expected her to share whatever she knew freely, but I can't blame her for being cautious after my appearance on the front page of the Jefferson County Tribune.

"I know she had the patience of a saint to put up with that man." Violet says finally. She sighs and looks back towards the house. "I'm still waiting for the damn girl to come out and offer drinks. Keep forgetting she's dead. Do you want a drink?"

"No, no, I'm fine, don't worry." I say.

"Good." Violet says. "I don't even know if there's anything in the fridge."

I smile, getting a better understanding of the work Lola did for Violet. It sounds like she was used as a housekeeper, or personal assistant, not a carer.

"So..." I encourage. "Nettie?"

"I don't know anything you won't already know, Connie. She was very tolerant, turning a blind eye to affair after affair."

"There was more than one?"

"Of course. Men like Desmond always have a woman on the side. I mean, she only discovered the truth of it the day he died. No, she's probably still discovering the truth of it. He was putting Lola up, you know that, paying all her bills. I don't know which one was to blame for that, he's never gone that far before. Could have been Lola pushing him for that."

"Blackmailing him." I say. A shiver runs through my body.

"Well, you know what, I guess she could have been. Never thought of it like that before." Violet says with a shake of her head. "What an awful business. They probably deserved each other."

"Maybe they're together now." I say.

Violet lets out a laugh. "I doubt it very much. He'll be watching Nettie like a hawk, won't want her to move on."

"What?"

"He was a very jealous man. Terrified she'd find someone else and leave him, realise she could do better. Not that he'd admit it, of course. Men who cheat are all the same. He'd got a beautiful woman, way out of his league, and he thought he'd cheat before she did."

"And did she?"

"Nettie?" Violet asks as her eyebrows jolt so high up her face they almost connect with her hairline. "Never. She's far too classy for that."

**

I head across town to Bill's, where I grab a trolley and feel the familiar frigid blast of air conditioning as I enter. I've learnt to always wear an extra layer when doing my weekly shop.

The supermarket is a yuppie's dream - Sage loves the place.

Organic this, hand-reared that. I roll my eyes as I walk past the spirulina and add a bag of potatoes to the trolley.

A man with a trolley full of frozen lobster and nothing else strolls past me in shorts and sandals. The hairs on his legs stand to attention. *First timer.*

Bill's does it's best to look like an independent, high-end retail store, but it's just the expensive arm of a huge super-market chain.

I turn up the next aisle, where I need to fight my way

through at least 86 different varieties of organic granola to find some good old fashioned corn flakes, and bang into a woman with electric blonde hair and the sweet scent of honeysuckle emanating from her.

Devin Summer.

"I'm so sorry!" I exclaim.

I haven't come across the supermodel since her much-talked-about arrival in town a few months earlier, but I know it's her because I've seen her face every day on the huge billboard that features her face not once but twice. On the left side, her chin is raised, her eyes closed. On the right, her chin is lowered and she stares off to the side. In both, she appears to be topless, although the camera only shows down to her shoulders. She's all scapula, clavicle and humerus.

The billboard was here (advertising a perfume that definitely isn't honeysuckle) before she was, and some of the townfolk were sent in a spin at the thought of a supermodel sharing their locale.

The excitement has died down now, and Devin keeps herself to herself.

She turns to look at me and I try not to gasp as I find myself looking at a real life supermodel. She's striking, that's for sure, but I wouldn't call her beautiful. Or attractive, really. You'd look twice at her, sure, but I think she almost looks like an alien. There's something not quite human about her eyes; something unseeing, or maybe too seeing.

A chill runs through me.

"I didn't see you." I blurt out, which must be something she's not used to hearing. I want her to do something to make this less awkward, but she just stands there. I realise after a few dumb moments of silence that I'm not just picking up on my nerves, I'm feeling her emotions as well. Sadness radiates from her. I feel an overwhelming desire to put as much space as I can between us.

"Are you okay?" I ask. What can I say? I'm a helper.

Devin makes eye contact with me and I force myself not to look away.

"Yes." She says. Her accent is clipped, impossible to trace. I believe she's American with Scandinavian roots. "You're the psychic?"

"Medium... yes." I say, then hold my hand out. "Connie Winters."

Devin allows me to shake her hand, and I become aware of her painful body proportions. Her wrists are almost the same circumference as my thumbs. "Devin Summer."

"Oh, we've got half the seasons covered, girl!" I exclaim with a stage laugh.

Devin gives a nod. She's clearly not in a rush to move away, so I push my trolley forwards.

"Bye for now." I say, and even offer a little wave, just to prove that I am a complete loser.

"Well, that went well." Sage says, appearing by my side. I should have known she wouldn't miss the chance to look around Bill's. "Did you see her trolley?"

I shake my head. I'd been too busy watching - and feeling - *her* to notice her shopping.

"Vegan." Sage whispers. She flashes me a knowing look but I'm not sure what she's trying to prove. "I was vegan too."

"For like two days." I mutter under my breath. Vegans are one of my pet hates. Not that I have anything against people who voluntarily give up cheese, apart from thinking they must be mad. But they're all so damn pious about it. Like veganism is three steps further up the ladder of enlightenment than the rest of us mere mortals, and they just can't step reminding everyone about it. Ugh.

"Erm, it was at least a month. And you try being vegan with two little kids who just want to eat cheeseburgers at every meal."

I smile. She'd told me by eMail that she had adopted an exciting new lifestyle - VEGANISM!!! (the capitals and the exclamation marks hers, not mine) - and by the time I'd replied to her message, still awkward with a computer and going weeks without even glancing at my eMail account, she'd returned to the dark side. "How are the girls?"

"Oh, fine." Sage says. I never mention her daughters unless she does. "I went over last night."

"Good." I say. "Any gossip?"

She shakes her head. She looks tired.

Spirits can move around the human world freely in theory, but every journey tires them. Sage visits the girls - well, they're women now - in England as often as she can, but always returns here tired and a little grumpy. I'll give her space for a day or two and then she'll update me, talking at a hundred miles an hour. I love those updates.

"Devin didn't look very happy for a supermodel." I say, changing the subject to safer ground until she's ready to talk.

"Supermodels have to be a bit miserable, don't they? For their art."

"Art?" I repeat.

Sage nods. "They treat it very seriously."

I shake my head. "The world's gone mad when that's what we think is a serious job."

Sage laughs and the sound feels like that first chunk of chocolate: so pure, delicious, and not enough. It's my favourite sound in the world. She stops though, as we head towards the check outs, where a large clock hangs on the wall.

"Is that the time?" She asks. "We have to go, Patton will be waiting."

11

SAGE

I cannot believe that Connie has made me late. I thought *I* was the disorganised one.

I float into the room, hoping for some kind of miracle that has made Patton run late, and can't believe it when I see the empty attic and realise my prayers have been answered.

"We're very lucky." I say as Connie follows behind me.

She takes a seat at the back of the room and I float next to her.

When Patton arrives, he's stressed as hell. His cheeks are bright red and he barely glances at us. Atticus floats in behind him and won't meet our gaze.

"What's wrong?" I ask.

"Ugh." Atticus groans. "Spirits can be the worst."

"What's happened?"

"They're complaining that Lola hasn't crossed over to us."

"She hasn't?" Connie asks, interested now.

Patton shakes his head. "Nobody's seen her."

"Wow." Connie says. It's standard procedure that a person crosses over into the spirit realm at the point where they died. It's actually a pretty flawed system, because if you die on holiday, you can end up stranded in some strange place with spirits you don't know until you learn how to move around. But that's the system, and everyone follows it. It can be hacked, of course, everything can. But nobody does it. Except, apparently, Lola.

"We can't blame her, really. One of the people here did kill her, after all." I say. "And she has no family, no real friends, here."

"That's not the point. The rules need to be followed." Atticus says. "I've got spirits out there now scared that this is going to start a trend. It could be mayhem."

"That's a little dramatic."

"I know that!" Atticus cries. "But try telling the crowd."

I shrug. I've got enough responsibility with the murder investigation. I'm not going to volunteer to keep the spirits happy as well.

"Connie." I say. "Can you talk to them?"

"Me?" She asks. "Why me?"

"They listen to you."

She rolls her eyes but doesn't refuse.

"Anyway." Patton says, clearing his throat to get our attention. "We're here to talk about the investigation, so let's forget about that other stuff for a while."

"Sure." I say. I sound like the teacher's pet and I don't even care. I want to impress Patton. His arm muscles may or may not have anything to do with that.

"Does anyone have any developments?"

"Well." Connie begins. "I've found out some interesting things about Lola."

"Excellent. Tell us more."

"She was blackmailing Desiree Montag."

Patton raises his eyebrows. "What a piece of work."

"I know. And I think she might have been blackmailing Desmond Frasier as well."

I laugh. "She was having an affair with him, he was perfectly willing I'm sure."

"Oh, of course." Connie says with a swat of her hand. "But he was also paying for her rent and everything, even though she was earning good money working for Violet. I think he had to pay her or she'd tell Nettie."

I screw up my nose. "I don't buy that. Nettie knew, surely."

"I don't think so." Connie says. "Not until just before his death."

"The tragic case of falling down the stairs just as your wife discovers your infidelity." Atticus says. "Such a sad accident."

The rumours of the truth being that Nettie had pushed him down the stairs after discovering the affair had done the rounds in the town, of course, but nobody seriously thought Nettie would lower herself to such an action.

"We should be considering her as a suspect." I say.

Atticus looks at me over his narrow glasses. "Nettie? Of course not."

"She wasn't at the funeral." Connie says.

"I'm sure she stayed away out of respect." Atticus says. He always had a soft spot for Nettie, with her classic beauty and immaculate appearance. The worse her life got, the more well-put-together she appeared.

"I don't seriously think she killed Desmond, but the fact that her husband and his other woman are both dead is a little suspicious, don't you think." I say.

Patton strokes his chin and nods. "You're right, Sage. We need to keep an eye on her. If it is her, she's probably feeling safe because there's no police around. She might slip up, make mistakes. I'll take a look at the file around Desmond's death."

Connie gasps. "The police were involved?"

"Yes, ma'am. There was no evidence it was anything other than an accident, but I'll be honest, everyone was so sure Nettie was innocent, it wasn't the most thorough investigation."

"Wow." She says. "I can't believe we're talking about people from Mystic Springs this way. I can't believe there's a murderer out there."

"Or in here." Patton says, looking across at Connie.

Her face blanches. "What?"

"I'm joking." Patton says with a booming laugh.

"Not appropriate." Atticus chastises.

Patton coughs. "Okay, anything else?"

None of us reply.

"Meeting dismissed, same time tomorrow." Patton says.

"Erm, Connie, I have a meeting with you shortly. I won't be late." Atticus says. Atticus is never late.

"Ok." Connie says.

"Sage, can I talk to you?" Patton asks.

"Sure." I say, trying to play it cool. "I have a few minutes."

He waits until Atticus and Connie have left; Connie flashing me a curious glance as she leaves. I shrug my shoulders.

"What is it?" I ask. He'd better not be about to throw me off the investigation team.

"I just wanted to say how impressed I am with you." He says. He's such a fine specimen of a spirit, and even better up close. Hand me a straw and I could drink him up all day. "With your work, I mean. You're doing a good job."

"Better than you expected, hey." I tease, aware of the flirtation in my voice. I decide to go the whole way and begin to twirl a strand of my dark hair too.

"It's been quite the revelation getting to know you better." He admits and I feel my insides flip, which is pure imagination because I don't have insides any more.

"Well, sure." I say, struggling to remember how to find words and form them.

"Are you okay?" He asks.

I nod, but the room is beginning to spin. I know what that means. I'm zoning.

Luckily, Patton has been a spirit enough himself to recognise the signs, and he calls for Connie, who hears the emergency in his tone and runs up the house and into the attic. She takes one look at me and lets out a low gasp.

"Is she zoning?"

Patton nods. He could deal with this, there's nobody who understands zoning better than another spirit, but I love that he has called for my sister. I try to say that to him but only random nonsensical words leave my mouth.

"Lie down." Connie commands.

I'm already on my way, lowering myself slowly because the whole world is spinning. It feels like a few of my evenings as a teenager, when I experimented with as much as I could fit in before my 9pm curfew and then returned home and pretended I didn't feel high as a kite or low as an anchor.

"You've done too much." She chastises as soon as I'm horizontal.

I know, I think. Returning to Waterfell Tweed to see my daughters is always draining, but so worth it. What I don't usually do is come home and work on a murder investigation.

"If she needs to leave the investigation, that's fine." Patton says.

"No!" I manage to cry out.

"Okay, well then you have to rest. You're no use to anyone if you're zoning."

I try to nod but I can feel my energy slipping. Zoning might just be the spirit equivalent of fainting, but every time it happens I get scared that I might disappear altogether. Every Halloween the spirits share No-More-Ghost Stories, about the things that have happened to spirits to stop them being spirits. Nobody seems to know if there's truth in the stories of spirits who got so lost during the crossover from being human that they're stuck in a strange limbo, or the ones so bad they were banished from being a spirit altogether, but the ones that have always terrified me are the tales of the zoners who zoned so badly they disintegrated completely.

I try to pull my mind back from those stories because nothing good comes from my focus being there.

Instead, I picture my girls. Sandy, with hair as dark as mine, and a personality as sweet as the cakes she bakes. And Coral, red hair to match her fieriness. I can still remember their weight in my lap as little girls, always busy, darting from one thing to the next, while I tried to work out how I could balance motherhood with still making sure my life was a grand adventure. They'd spot me sometimes, gazing at nothing when I should have been watching the umpteenth performance of their made-up dance routine and reacting as if I'd just witnessed Swan Lake for the first time.

I knew I wasn't the best mum in the world, but I tried to be the best mum I could in the moments when I had the energy for it. Like the time they wanted a disco and I moved the kitchen table out into the garden, in the rain, so we could use the kitchen as a dance floor. We turned the music up loud that summer, dancing to Bob Dylan and John Lennon, the girls each wearing a tie-dye t-shirt of mine that dropped to the floor like a maxi dress, and when we realised the kitchen table was ruined, I grabbed a huge patchwork blanket from my own childhood and declared it the year of picnics.

The neighbours weren't impressed with me that summer, between the eyesore of the table in the garden and the loud music, but my house was full of laughter. Maybe this could be a grand adventure, I thought. Maybe this is the grand adventure of my life. To raise these girls. To dance until I feel the music in my bones. To laugh until my stomach muscles hurt.

"Stay with us." Connie's voice calls to me as if through a fog. I open my eyes and try to find her, try to focus in on her curls. Instead I see Patton, his chiseled jaw, those blue blue eyes. I stare at him, conscious enough to hope I'm giving him a sultry stare rather than a murderous glare, and patches of the room start to come into focus again. The spinning slows.

I laugh.

"Just stay quiet... and still." Connie says.

I blink and find her face. I count her chins and think about how I love each of them. I could even give them nicknames, I ponder.

Zoning is a little like coming down from a drug trip, so I hear. It makes sense. I feel giddy, but tired.

"We'll have to talk about you getting more rest." Connie is saying, but I don't want to listen any more.

I close my eyes and let the tiredness wash over me. Faces flash into my mind as I allow myself to rest.

"I love you." I mumble, like a drunk. I don't know if I'm

saying it out loud. Nobody replies but I don't mind. I feel surrounded by love. And I love myself. That's the emptiness I was trying to fill with adventure for the longest time.

Love.

"It's all about love." I murmur, knowing I'm on the brink of discovering the secret to life and happiness and that I won't be able to tell anyone about it. How can I explain it? It suddenly feels urgent that I open my eyes. I force them open and sit up.

Connie and Patton stand by me, their faces etched with concern.

"You're back." Connie says, fighting tears away.

"That was a bad one." Patton says.

I grin at them, feeling as happy as I can ever remember, and they glance at each other and then back at me, before we all burst out laughing.

It's a crazy, crazy time to be a ghost.

12

CONNIE

"*I*'m sure she's just a few minutes late." I say as Atticus floats from one side of the room to the other, his arms behind his back. It's ten past the hour and unlike Mariam to be late. So much of her life is built on routine, predictability and rules she must follow to stay on the right path.

Finally, there's a knock at the door and I pad across the house.

"Hello, come in." I welcome.

Mariam rolls her eyes and walks in, pulling her muddy rain boots off and leaving them by the door.

"Been riding?" I ask.

She shakes her head. "Can't get in the habit of wearing proper shoes."

I smile. Horses were Mariam's life, until Atticus fell from one and died. The equestrian dream was ruined for her then, but she's never stopped dressing like a rider. She wears dark skinny jeans, a checked shirt and a body warmer. Even her socks have cartoons on of someone showjumping.

"Your dad's here already." I whisper.

"Of course." She says.

I've already set out the water on the table and I gesture for her to take a seat.

Mariam has been so often she doesn't have to bring an item that belonged to Atticus.

"Okay." I say as I lower myself into the settee. It's starting to sag and I adjust my frame on it as I feel what I imagine to be a spring poking up through the fabric. It will need replacing soon. "Mariam, your father is already here. Do you have any questions to begin?"

Mariam shakes her head. I start every session this way because once Atticus begins speaking, and grilling her, there won't be a chance for her to interrupt.

"Atticus?" I ask.

He's sitting next to Mariam on the settee, which might freak her out, so I do my usual and close my eyes while I talk to him. People think that part is for dramatic effect, but the truth is, it would be unsettling for my customers to see my eyes wander as I follow the spirit around the room.

"Ask her if she's dry." He says. I groan. I wish there was a way of me talking to him without Mariam hearing.

I take a deep breath and rephrase. This job's like being a politician sometimes. "He wants to know how your recovery is going."

Mariam cocks her head to one side and ponders the question. "It's going well." She admits. "I'm staying plugged into the meetings, and I'm feeling good."

"That's excellent." I say.

"I don't feel like I'm being chased by demons quite as much." She says with a sad smile. "And then I feel guilty. Why is it fair for me to enjoy life if dad can't."

"Nonsense." Atticus barks. "Is she riding again?"

"Your dad says you shouldn't feel like that." I say. "He asks if you're riding again."

She shakes her head. "I can't."

"She needs to. She's far too talented to just give up." Atticus says. He is watching her, his translucent face just inches from hers. She shivers at one point, and he moves back slightly.

"Your dad says you're so talented, it's a shame not to ride."

Mariam scoffs. "Remind him I was the one who found him and tried to resuscitate him while the ambulance took its time. I've seen what a horse can do to you. My riding days are over."

I swallow. It's so sad. The paint horses they had loved, with their pinto spotting patterns, were transformed from friend to foe in that instant for Mariam.

"I worry that she needs to keep busy." Atticus says.

"Your dad wants you to keep busy."

"I am." She says with a laugh. "I'm here all the time speaking to him."

She looks at me then and I see the pain in her eyes. She regrets the words. When her father died, she ran to me instead of the hospital, knowing that he was gone. She sat and sobbed on that very settee while I, foolishly, poured her glass of wine after glass of wine. I'm not suggesting I created her alcohol problem, but I certainly didn't help. That's why I created the water only rule.

He hadn't turned up that day. Atticus Hornblower was so focused on his town, and his daughter - probably in that order - that his passing over wasn't easy. He clung to the living world, not realising that he was eagerly awaited by the spirits. If there was a limbo that spirits could be sucked into, as the spirits like to gossip about, Atticus Hornblower found it as he did his best to simply refuse to die.

"I didn't mean that. Sorry, dad." Mariam says. "He's right. You're right, dad. I do need to keep busy. And I am. Work is always busy."

Atticus frowns by her side. "Tell her to be careful of Desiree."

I glance at him and try to shrug - *why?*

"Tell her, she's a suspect in a murder case."

I let out a low sigh. Desiree is Mariam's boss. I'm fairly sure it would be breaking a million rules to reveal to Mariam that she's being considered a murder suspect.

"Your dad worries that Desiree isn't a good influence."

Mariam's body stiffens. "Why?"

"He won't say." I lie.

"Yes I will!" Atticus barks. "Tell her! She needs to be warned."

I sigh. "He just asks that you be careful."

Mariam's cheeks flush red and she shakes her head. "You know, maybe the time has come for me to move forward with my life."

"What does she mean?" Atticus asks.

"What do you mean?" I repeat.

Mariam takes a sip of water and picks up her saddle bag from the carpet, then gets up to her feet. "Daddy. I love you and I miss you. I'm not sure these meetings are the best way for me to move forward with my life."

"What's she doing?" Atticus asks. He remains on the settee and, as he gazes up at his daughter, suddenly looks old and very afraid.

"Mariam." I begin. "You're free to leave, of course, but are you okay?"

She glares at me with such ferocity I can't believe I ever

had the misconception that she was my almost best-friend. I barely know her really. I just know her slightly better than I know anyone else.

"I'm not going home to get drunk, if that's what you mean." She spits at me. Even in her full blown addiction stage, I never saw her like this.

"It isn't." I lie. "I just don't want you to go home and be upset. I'm sure your dad would leave us to it if you want to stay and have a chat."

"So you can report back to him?" Mariam asks. "Or so he can float around in the next room and listen? No. I'm done here. I just want to be on my own."

I nod and follow her to the door, where we spend an awkward few moments not speaking to each other while she puts her riding boots back on. She opens the door herself and leaves without saying goodbye.

Atticus is on the settee, head in his hands.

"I'm sorry." I say.

"I thought she'd grown out of that." He says with a sigh. "We had blazing rows when she was younger. She's too much like me, that's the problem. We argue because we both know we're right and the other one's wrong. Oh, I've ruined it all. What if she doesn't come back?"

I walk through to the kitchen and make myself a strong coffee. "Maybe some space isn't a bad idea."

He looks at me, wounded by my words.

"This set up, it isn't typical. Regular meetings... I know why you've wanted to do it, but maybe it is keeping Mariam from moving on fully."

Atticus groans. "I worry about the girl."

"I know." I say. Everyone worries about Mariam. Or at least they did, back when she was holding up the bar every night and when her eyes were more bloodshot than white. But, she seems to have straightened herself out now.

"I'd feel better if she'd stay away from Desiree."

"Why?"

"She's a murder suspect!"

I frown. "There's a few suspects, you didn't warn her away from anyone else."

"She doesn't spend time with any of the others." Atticus says. "She works with Desiree. She could be in danger."

"Look, what if I go and speak to Desiree, would that make you feel better?"

He jumps up from the settee and begins to pace the room again. "Don't mention Mariam."

"Of course not." I say with a laugh. "Why would I?"

Atticus doesn't laugh. He looks down at the floor for a moment before answering. "I just want to protect my baby girl."

"Okay, well, leave it to me. I'll go and talk to Desiree."

Atticus nods and then leaves. I tidy the consultation room and close the doors, then walk out to the veranda and sit on my rocking chair with what's left of my coffee.

The neighbourhood is quiet. It's the middle of the day, people are at work or school. Shift workers are catching up on sleep.

An old Honda Civic drives by slowly and I raise my hand and wave to the unknown driver. That's the kind of place this is.

After that, nothing.

I sip my drink and try to clear my mind. I don't blame Mariam for considering cutting back the contact with Atticus. I've wondered how healthy it is for a while.

I wonder if I was irresponsible for allowing the monthly meetings to go on as long as they have. I haven't earned anything from it, though, Mariam can't pay me on her teacher's salary. And it was Mariam who wanted the regular contact. When she was going through withdrawal, her dad's words gave her enormous strength.

Now, she seems not to need him. That could be time passing, of course, healing the grief.

But I don't buy it.

I think something else is going on.

I think Mariam is hiding something.

13

CONNIE

I decide to walk down to the coffee house and see if my hunch is right.

People are creatures of habit. If you stop by the coffee house for coffee one day, there's a good chance it's part of your routine and you'll do it again the next day.

"Hey, Connie." Ellie says, her voice barely more than a whisper.

"You ok?"

She nods. "Got this annoying croak in my throat."

"Ugh, I hate that." I say, which is true. I'm a total baby when I get sick. "Hope you're taking care of yourself?"

She shrugs and I laugh. She's a small business owner, she'll look after herself when she can afford to hire staff or take a holiday.

Godiva, the Persian cat, glares at me from her bed on the floor.

"Ignore her." Ellie whispers. "She's such a grump."

"She's got a good life, sitting in here all day, hearing all the gossip."

Ellie gazes down at Godiva and smiles in that way that

only cat lovers understand. "I like being able to see her. She makes me smile, even on the days when it seems like everyone's a nut job who wants to make my life hell."

I laugh at her honesty. "Gotta love working with the public, hey."

She rolls her eyes. "It's a total dream. You want a cappuccino?"

"Please, honey." I say.

The coffee house is quiet. In the furthest corner from the door, there's a man in shorts and a hoodie working on a laptop. His table is full of empty takeout cups, and his earbuds drown out the coffee house's music selection. Close to the window is a young mum with a sleeping baby in a huge pushchair. She raises the enormous mug of coffee to her lips and her face is practically transformed by the miracle of the moment: a hot drink, in peace. No sooner does she put her mug down than laptop man's phone rings, the heavy R'n'B ringtone waking the baby instantly. The woman glares across at him, then meets my eye and shares an eye roll with me before scooping the baby out of the pushchair.

"Sprinkles?" Ellie asks.

"Nah, I'm good." I say. I never see the point of chocolate sprinkles on a cappuccino. They add nothing to the taste but increase the calories. Not that I'm watching my calories, or my weight, but I have to draw the line somewhere, and chocolate sprinkles is it.

I wander across towards a table near the woman with the fussing baby and offer her a smile.

"Literally my first hot drink in six weeks." She says, and I realise that the pushchair houses two babies, not one. One remains, somehow, fast asleep. She notices me taking in the full reality and grimaces. "Oh, she's fine. It's always him. Such a light sleeper, aren't you boo?"

The baby boy quiets as soon as she places the dummy in his mouth.

"Will he go back in there now?" I ask.

"It's not worth the risk." She says with a small laugh. She struggles to reach for her drink, given its size and weight, while holding the baby.

"I could hold him." I say, my words surprising me. I love babies. "I mean, I know I'm a stranger, so that's probably a little odd for me to offer. But if you want to enjoy your drink…"

"You know, that would be so nice. Come and join me." She says. I manoeuvre the pushchair slightly so I can squeeze past it and sit across from her, then she hands me the tiny baby, who doesn't stir as he is transferred into my arms. It's been a long time since I've held a baby, but it comes right back to me; how to support the head; how, after a while, my arm begins to ache and I need to rest my crooked elbow against the arm of the chair. I manage to avoid the temptation to inhale that new baby scent from his head; that would be *too* weird.

"Your babies are so beautiful."

"Oh, thanks. They say mothers are biased, but I think they are too."

I grin at her. "I'm Connie, by the way."

"Adele." She replies. "We just moved here."

"Oh, well welcome! Whereabouts have you moved from?"

"New York." Adele says, curling her nose up. "I adored that place, until I found out we were pregnant. I didn't want to raise a family in such a huge city. Taylor, my husband, he's been waiting for a transfer to come up."

"Well, this place definitely isn't a huge city. Although you'd think so with how good this coffee is."

"This place is super cute." Adele says, glancing around the interior of the coffee house. "I can see me being here a whole lot, especially if these two learn to sleep at the same time and give me some peace."

"What's it like?" I ask. "Having twins? I've always wondered how people cope."

She sighs. "It's a little bit like being put through one of those sleep deprivation tortures, but by the most beautiful, perfect scientist in the world, who you're madly in love with. Like, it's hell, but you're also kind of grateful every time you're woken up because it gives you chance to see them again."

I laugh. "That's a pretty good way to explain it. Shall I just shut up so you can drink in peace?"

Adele shakes her head. "Oh no, trust me, adult company is very appreciated right now."

"You're not with..." I start, wondering how to politely ask if she's a single mum, even though she mentioned her husband earlier.

"Taylor's finishing up work in New York. He'll be joining us in a few weeks. So, I have a couple months of loneliness ahead of me."

"Oh no." I protest. "You know me now. And I'll introduce you to everyone else, they're all friendly. Trust me, Mystic Springs is not a place to worry about being lonely. You'll be fine."

"You're the sweetest, Connie. Thank you." She says. The baby boy begins to squirm in my arms, just as she finishes the last of her drink. She reaches out her arms and takes him from me, instinctively raising his butt to her nose, which she crinkles after taking a smell. "Ooh, Mr, you are such a stinker. We need to get you changed."

I smile politely, and notice Desiree walk in.

"Will you excuse me? I need to get this one changed and then we should head home. It was so great to meet you."

"Oh, of course, the toilets are right in the back there. Do you need a hand with the door or anything?"

"I'll be okay." Adele says with a laugh. "I'm finally starting to figure things out. Let's do this again, though? Here, have my card. That sounds so pompous, I apologise, but I don't know my number otherwise."

She hands me a glossy business card. *Adele Morton, Attorney at Law* it reads. "I'll text you my number."

I sit and sip my cappuccino as she bundles her babies off towards the toilet. I can already feel the ache in my arm from holding the baby boy.

A few moments later, Desiree joins me.

"I thought you'd hidden your pregnancy very well for a moment, then." She says with a smile.

I return the smile, ignoring the temptation to make some reply about how it's easy to hide a pregnancy when you're the size of a house anyway. She's clearly being friendly, and I'm not the size of a house. Not really.

"No babies here. How about you? You never wanted to give Troy a brother or sister?"

She shakes her head quickly. "He was a terrible baby. I don't remember anything about my life before him, but if I *had* wanted more than one child, he cried and screamed and convinced me to forget that idea."

"Oh, dear." I say. "You'd never know that to look at him now. He seems like such an old spirit."

She nods. "He's a good kid. But he can have his moments still. Can't we all?"

"How's he holding up?" I ask.

Desiree shrugs. "He doesn't seem that affected. He didn't really know Lola."

"It seems like nobody did." I murmur.

Desiree shakes her head and takes a sip of her iced tea.

I imitate her actions and take a long drink of my cappuccino, wondering how to question her without her realising what I'm doing. Subtlety has never been my strongest skill.

"Are you ok, Connie?" She asks, her brow furrowed with concern.

I nod a little too vigorously. I'm going to have to get creative. "I'm finding it hard to sleep. Aren't you?"

"Because of Lola?" Desiree asks. "Well, no, actually."

"Oh." I say. Strike one, I think. The person with the least to fear is the murderer.

"I think Lola was targeted." Desiree continues. "I know that's an awful thing to say, but I don't think we suddenly have a serial killer among us."

"What makes you say that?"

Desiree shrugs. "All the history we have without a murder? I have to believe there was some reason here."

"But how can you be so confident there won't be a reason to hurt someone else?" I ask, stopping myself from adding, *unless you're the killer.*

"What reason could there be?" She throws the question back at me. "Lola wasn't close to anyone. She wasn't involved in the community. There's nothing that links her to another person enough to put them at risk."

"Oh." I say. It makes sense, although I was never too concerned about being a target. Perhaps, like Desiree, I'd been reassured by how separate Lola seemed.

"Ya know, I've been thinking, did someone from her past catch up with her?" Desiree asks.

I meet her gaze and she raises her eyebrows for impact. "Wow, I hadn't considered that."

Desiree shrugs. "I did some digging. Turns out she's wanted in Alabama."

"No way." I gasp.

"Mm-hmm." Desiree says, sadness plaguing her face. Every young person who falls through the cracks pains her. "Grand theft auto."

"So she stole a car and came here on the run?" I ask. I don't remember Lola's arrival into the town, but I know I never saw her in a vehicle.

"I don't think so." Desiree says. "I think she was involved in something bigger. A gang, perhaps."

"No." I protest, considering how young Lola had seemed, despite her determination to appear - and act - as if she was older.

"I see it." Desiree says. "I like to think I know the signs."

I nod because I'm not the expert here. Desiree worked years in the inner city schools before moving out here to give her and Troy - Troy especially - a better quality of life.

"So somebody could have followed her here? But why?"

She shrugs. "Any number of reasons. She could have had information someone didn't want her to. She could have owed somebody something. She could even have tipped off the cops on someone. Maybe she'd been black-mailing someone else and they decided enough was enough. When you move in those circles, there's a lot of reasons to take a life."

"What was she blackmailing you about, again?" I ask, trying for casual disinterest, as if I've forgotten that she's already dodged the question once.

Desiree watches me and bites her lip. "Something private."

I finish my cappuccino and sit back in the chair. Lola had information about Desiree. Information that I see, even now, Desiree wants to protect. If she's guilty, the best thing to do is make someone else look guilty.

"So what are the signs?" I ask.

She blinks.

"Of gang involvement, or whatever? I'm just curious."

Desiree sighs. "You know I spoke to her about enrolling? She wasn't interested. Just not open to it at all. But she spent the whole time doodling. I always leave pen and paper out when I'm talking to a student, ya know, some people listen better when their hands are busy, and some kids can't keep eye contact. So she doodled, said no way to school, and left. And I always check doodles, they can tell us so much. Hers were this crown, this five-pointed crown. Just again and again and again, all over the page."

"And that shows you're in a gang?"

"It can. It's one of the most common gang affiliation symbols. Obviously, it's not enough on its own, but it made me wonder." Desiree says with a frown. "I sure wish I'd pushed harder with her. It never gets easier, ya know, feeling like you're failing those kids."

I look at her and wonder what the heck I'm doing even considering she could have hurt Lola. She's devoted her entire life to helping kids, not harming them.

"You did what you could, and it was more than most of us." I admit. "It was so awful, seeing her end up like that..."

"I'm glad I wasn't there." She says. "I'm sorry, I'm not pleased you were there instead, I just can't imagine..."

"You weren't there?" I repeat, returning in my mind to the April Fool's party. I can't remember specifically seeing Desiree, but it had been busy.

She shakes her head. "I had a conference in the city."

"I thought Mariam usually went to those?" I ask. I know this because Mariam moans about the damn things every time they come around; whole days filled with reminders of things teachers never forget when they could do with the time to work on lesson plans and marking.

Desiree begins to pick the skin around her thumb nail. "I can't talk about that."

"What?"

"I can't talk about my staff." She says, in her principal's voice. "It's not appropriate."

"Okay..." I drawl. "I wasn't asking how much you pay her. I just, erm, it doesn't matter."

Desiree coughs and begins to gather up her things from around her. "I need to get going."

"Sure." I say awkwardly. "I hope I haven't upset you. I didn't mean..."

"Oh, hush." Desiree says with a grimace. "It's been nice to chat to you. I've probably just had too much caffeine."

I force a small laugh. "Take care of yourself."

"And you!" Desiree calls, and with that she's gone, taking whatever secrets she has with her.

14

SAGE

I like to visit in the evening, when they've kicked off their shoes and their responsibilities for the day and are just being themselves. They're not always together, especially now one of them has found a man. I want to scream at them: *don't put men before each other!*

Easy for me to say.

I never liked this place, with it's small community and the judging eyes I felt surrounded by. Surrounded by house-wives who were doing a better job than me at everything. Their whites were whiter, their cutlery was more polished, their doorsteps were swept more often than mine.

I felt their judgement weigh down on me like a pile of rubble, and I wanted to escape.

Then I looked at those two faces, those little faces who looked at me and saw sunshine and rainbows, and I cast aside the neighbours' opinions and grabbed them for another dance or took them out into the garden with a tub of water and a paintbrush each and let them decorate the back of the house.

This, I can do well, I would say.

And now, as I visit, I know that I did do it well. My whites were a little yellow, my cutlery might have had a smear here and there, and my doorstep was never swept, but my girls were happy. And they've grown to be amazing women.

I hover near the door, not wanting to attract any attention to my presence. I don't want to spook them.

Sandy brings in drinks, even though they're at Coral's house, which I could totally have predicted being the way things would work out for these two. Coral curls up on the settee and takes the mug of cocoa from her sister. She looks feline with her bright eyes and long limbs. Feline and tired. I hope she's been sleeping.

"Want a blanket?" Sandy offers, already pacing back across the room to grab the blanket that lives on the back of the armchair. She spreads it across Coral's slender legs then takes a seat herself.

"I'm so tired." Coral says. She closes her eyes for a moment, then opens them and yawns.

"Go to bed." Sandy says. "I'll have my drink and let myself out."

"No, no, it's been too long since we just sat and chatted. Talk to me... tell me everything."

Sandy laughs. "There's not much to tell."

"How are things with Tom?"

Sandy grins, as she always does when someone mentions her boyfriend's name. I don't blame her, he's quite a catch. "They're amazing. I think he's The One."

"Well, duh." Coral replies with an eye roll. "Of course he is. Have you only just figured that out?"

Sandy shivers. "Did you feel that?"

I realise I've moved forward, into the room, and as I feared, Sandy has felt my presence. Yes, it's possible. That cold draught you feel? It could be a spirit. Things being moved? Could be a spirit. That sense that you're being watched? Could be a spirit. Most living people are too cynical to pick up on those signs. The best people are children and the elderly, and nobody believes them, or people in a high state of emotion. Some people are just naturally more tuned in, like Connie.

"It's gone a bit cold." Coral agrees, pulling the blanket around her further. "The heating's probably turned off."

"Do you ever wonder if mum's watching us?" Sandy asks, and I gasp. I've never heard them talk about me, which is to be expected. I've been dead a long time. They can't be expected to sit around and remember me every night. But still. A mother can hope.

"Of course she is." Coral says with a firm nod.

"I like to think so too." Sandy says. "I mean, I don't want to see her, that would freak me the heck out. But I hope she knows we're okay. I hope she's proud of us."

I begin to cry. *I'm so proud of you, darling girls.*

"She is." Coral says. "Look at us, we're amazing."

Sandy laughs.

"But seriously, mum wouldn't just take dying as the end."

"Maybe that's the adventure she always dreamed of." Sandy says, and I realise she's right. I wanted an adventure, something bigger than me, and life gave me two perfect girls and mundane chores, but death gave me a grand adventure. A whole new world. And now, a murder investigation.

"If she was here, what would you say to her?" Coral asks.

I hold my breath.

"I'd tell her to be happy. And tell her we're happy. If I could speak for both of us. I think that's all that matters really." Sandy says.

"I'd tell her I love her, and I'd ask her to plait my hair again. Sitting with her, knowing I had all her attention, while she did my hair, that was the best feeling ever."

"Aww, come here." Sandy says, and Coral climbs out of her cocoon and sits by her sister's feet. Sandy takes a clump of her auburn hair. "I'm not very good at this."

My daughters descend into laughter as Sandy attempts to weave strands of Coral's hair into something resembling a plait. My fingers tingle with the desire to go across there and do it for her. After ten minutes, Sandy gives up, apologising for the mess she's made. The evening grows quiet and Sandy sees herself out when she notices that Coral has fallen asleep on the settee.

"Goodbye." I whisper as she walks out, and she stops for a moment. As if she's heard the ghost of a sound. She shakes her head, and leaves.

I float across to Coral and take three strands of her hair in my fingers, twisting each in turn. There's no elastic, the plait will probably have dropped out by morning, but it makes me smile.

"Goodnight." I whisper, but she has always been a deep sleeper, and my words don't reach her.

**

"She's hiding something." Connie says. "But I don't think she's the killer."

"How can we be sure if we don't unearth whatever she's hiding?" Atticus asks. We're gathered in the attic for our daily meeting and Connie is relaying her meeting with Desiree. I'm still on cloud nine from the visit to my girls last night, feeling a mix of regular post-visit tiredness and a happiness that would seep into my bones if I had any.

"We can't expect the whole town to share their secrets with us." I say with alarm. I imagine having to confess that I quite like looking at Patton. How embarrassing would that be?

"She's the principal of the school!" Atticus cries.

"Let's move on." Patton says. He keeps a meeting running smoothly, add that to his list of talents. "Connie, what makes you think she isn't the killer?"

"She was out of town."

"Oh." Atticus says. "Do we know that for sure?"

Connie nods. "She was at an education conference. I've checked online and there are photos from the night, she's clearly there. She was given an award, which she didn't mention to me, but it explains why she was there not Mariam."

"Mariam?" Atticus repeats.

"She seems to go to a lot of these conferences instead of Desiree, but obviously she couldn't go and collect the award."

"Yes." Atticus says. "She's always doing that woman's job for her. Late nights and early mornings, don't let anyone tell you teaching is easy."

"She mentioned some interesting things." Connie says, ignoring Atticus' rant. "Lola was wanted in Alabama for grand theft auto, and Desiree thinks she may have had some kind of gang involvement."

"Which means someone might have tracked her down." Patton says.

"Exactly." Connie says.

"Well, what chance do we have of solving this case if it's a stranger?" I ask.

"We're not giving up." Patton says.

"No, of course not." I say, not wanting to be the hopeless one. "I just mean, Sheriff, in your experience, how do you go about this type of investigation?"

Patton blushes slightly and his chest balloons out with pride. "Well, we continue investigating. Speak to people. Did anyone see a stranger around town, especially on that night? Who was in charge of letting people in at the party?"

Connie shakes her head. "Nobody, really. It was an open house, anyone could come."

Patton groans. "That makes it harder. But still, someone might remember seeing someone strange."

"Wouldn't they have reported it by now?"

"To who?" Atticus asks. "Rydell Grove and Jefferson County have left us out to dry. If they did receive any calls, we wouldn't know."

"That's a good point." Patton says. "Just because the calls aren't being dealt with doesn't mean they haven't happened. There will be a file, probably in both towns."

"So, shall I call them?" Connie asks.

"No." Patton says. "They won't tell you anything. I'll go."

"I'll come with you." I say, certain he will refuse the offer.

"That would be good." He says to my surprise. "Let's go tomorrow night."

I pretend to check my imaginary diary, then notice his frown. "Sure, that works for me."

"Any other business to discuss?" Patton asks.

"I'm still not sure how I feel about my daughter working for a woman who keeps secrets." Atticus says. He removes his glasses and wipes the inner corners of his eyes.

"That's not really police business, sir." Patton says. "We need to stay focused in these meetings."

"Well, could you at least look into her past a little?" Atticus asks. "Get her police record or something?"

"Absolutely not." Patton says. "We're in the middle of a murder investigation, the like of which the world has never seen before. This might be the first time spirits and humans have worked together to catch a killer. We'll have no suggestion that we've abused our powers to satisfy curiosity. Desiree Montag is a good woman."

Atticus lets out a sigh.

"What *is* your issue with her, Atticus?" Connie asks from beside me. She's done some crazy impression of a bun with her hair today and trust me, it is not working. I need to have a chat with her about how to flatter the shape of her face, and it's not by scraping her hair away to within an inch of it's life.

"It's just a feeling."

"Just a feeling?" Patton asks with an eyebrow raised. I start to tune out of the conversation so I can enjoy looking at him more, but these people are too noisy. Ain't no place in this town where a spirit can just sit back and admire an impressive ghostly specimen.

"In other news, have you guys had much to do with the supermodel?"

"Devin Summer?" I ask, because here's an interesting subject finally. "Of course. What do you want to know?"

"Nothing." Connie says with a laugh. "But as you know, Sage, I crossed paths with her recently, she's a little intense."

"She's an artist." I say. I've already explained this to her.

"She's a supermodel."

"That's her art." I say. I know I'm right because I've read a four-page interview with her. "She's very passionate about the art of modelling."

"So she gets paid to be attractive?" Patton asks.

"Hmm, I wouldn't say she's..." Connie begins.

"It's all about expression. She seems to be quite fascinating." I say. "I went to her house recently, her walk-in wardrobe is insane. I've never seen so many designer labels in one place."

Patton eyes me. "You were in her house?"

I gulp. "Just once, I swear. I'm sorry."

"You know the rules." Patton says. "I assume she didn't invite you in?"

"Well, no... but I did hear her crying. I wouldn't have gone in otherwise."

"She was upset when I saw her too." Connie says. "Was she okay?"

"She was just in bed sobbing. I watched her for a while, but she didn't seem like she was going to hurt herself, and I didn't know what I could do, so I left. I may have got lost on the way out and ended up in her wardrobe. For just a moment."

"I bet her house is amazing."

"It is." I admit. "It's strange, she has all these photos up, of herself. I mean, good for her, but I wouldn't want my face looking back at me like that."

15

SAGE

*I*t's the middle of the night and the streets are empty; houses cast in covers of darkness. A lone owl hoots at us from the branches of a sugar maple. Even the spirits, who tend to be more comfortable in the twilight hours, have turned in for the night.

"Are you sure this is a good idea?" I ask.

Connie turns to me and rolls her eyes. She's wearing the lycra yoga pants that were on sale that year she decided she should exercise more, and they're unforgiving on her lumps and bumps. I try to avert my eyes. I must remember to find them later and throw them in the trash.

"Here." She says, and hands a small hammer to me. I don't move. "Take it, it'll be quicker if we both do it."

I groan and take the hammer and promptly drop it on the sidewalk. It clatters, and that earns me a glare from Connie.

"It's too heavy." I object. Spirits can touch things, but we have to practice. When we're newly crossed over, we float through everything, and we have to train our muscles to touch something, grip it, pick it up. I've got decades of practice behind me so I can pick things up without thinking, and float through other things as I need to, but I never had an interest in DIY when I was living, I certainly haven't developed one since. The hammer is just too heavy.

"Fine, you can hold the paper." Connie says. She passes me a sheet of paper and gestures to the sugar maple, where the owl watches us with interest. I pin the sheet up at around eye level, and hold it in place while Connie hammers a single nail through it. I'm sure I can feel the tree wince with every knock.

"How far apart are we doing these?" I ask. Connie's printed a stack of the flyers. I can see a long night ahead of us.

"We'll start with a few each street, I'd rather cover as much of town as possible than flyer every tree on two streets." Connie says.

The flyers were her idea, stolen shamelessly from real investigations. Flyers asking for anonymous tips.

The next thing I knew, she was setting up a generic email address and designing these flyers that call for anyone with information about Lola's death to share what they can, either with their name or anonymously.

"We'll do this one." Connie says and I hold another flyer in place while she hammers a nail through it.

"I went to see the girls." I say as we move through the streets quickly. Although we don't say it, neither of us want to be out after dark while a killer remains loose.

"I thought so. You've been tired. That's probably why you couldn't hold the hammer."

"You think?" I ask. That hadn't occurred to me. "I just thought I wasn't used to something that heavy."

Connie shrugs. "Maybe."

"Well?" I prompt.

"Huh?"

"Don't you want to know how they are?"

Connie rolls her eyes. "Of course I do, give me chance to ask. I'm concentrating on the best spots for these flyers too."

"Are you okay?" I ask. It's unlike her to be so snappy, and disinterested. She's never been a part of the girls' life, and we both regret that now. I wish she'd go and visit them, see them for herself, but she's convinced they wouldn't be interested in her. Or would be angry that she waited so long.

"I'm fine." Connie snaps. "Go on, tell me how they are."

I don't answer. To my surprise, I begin to silently cry.

Immediately, Connie stops and looks at me, and I catch my breath and stop crying.

"You knew I was crying." I say.

She nods, and I see how tired she looks.

"What's going on?" I ask.

She takes a deep breath. "It's been happening more and more. It's like I can, like, feel people's emotions. It's freaking me the heck out."

I burst into a grin. "This is so cool!"

"It's really not, trust me."

"No, listen to me." I say. "It's okay. I can do it too."

Connie rolls her eyes. "Just for once, can the conversation be about me, Sage?"

"Wow." I say. "You are so annoying."

"And you're so self-centred."

"Me? You're the one who ran away from your family."

"How dare you!" She whispers. You know she's really angry when she whispers.

"You couldn't handle living in my shadow." I say. This is a repeat of every argument we've had since she left Waterfell Tweed. I know my lines without even concentrating.

"I was only ever in your shadow in your own head." She

says. "Can we stay focused on the job we're doing?"

And so we continue moving through the empty streets, disturbing the occasional cat, causing the odd porch light to switch on as we pass. I hold the flyers, she hammers, and we snip at each other like only sisters can.

"It's not my fault I'm the pretty one." I say.

She glares at me. "Do you know how annoying it is that you'll never age? It's just so typical of you to get to die while you're still young and beautiful."

"I'm sorry you hate me so much." I say. This is my argument-ender. She can't stay angry when I throw this line in.

"You're insane." She says, and I see her face soften. I feel the tightness in her chest relax. I can literally sense the red anger seep out of her body, leaving her with a blue aura of calm. I feel those things, even if she doesn't believe me.

"So, you want me to explain to you what you're feeling?" I ask.

She nods as she hammers in another flyer and crosses the street so we can start looping back towards home.

"You're an empath." I say. "It's a real thing, I've had it for as long as I can remember."

"You're serious?" She asks and I nod. "Does it freak you out?"

"It's really not a big deal. For a long time, I thought everyone could do it. It's not like I can read thoughts, it's just general emotions. So I know if someone's happy or sad. Is that how it is for you?"

"I don't know." Connie says. "It's only started recently. It's more that I've picked up a dark energy around a few people. That sounds terrifying. I felt it from Devin Summer."

"Oh, yeah. Totally." I agree. "There's nothing terrifying there, though. That's pure grief."

"I just wanted to get away from her when I felt it."

Connie admits. "I couldn't have said it was grief, just something I didn't want to be near."

"You'll tune in to it more." I say.

"I'm not sure I want to."

"Well, I don't think you can just switch it off. And it can be quite handy. Trust me."

"It feels like I'm intruding on people's thoughts." Connie says. "I don't want to know how people feel, unless they want to tell me. I'm already worn out by dealing with everything else."

I hold up the last flyer and Connie nails it in to the wooden noticeboard outside the church. "Job's done." I say and stifle a yawn.

A light flicks on in a bedroom window of a house as we pass. We both instinctively look up towards the light. A blond woman cocooned in a white dressing gown stands in front of the window, bends down, scoops up a baby and begins to pace back and forth in the room.

"She's new." I say.

"I've spoken to her." Connie says. "Adele. She's here on her own with twin babies until her husband joins them."

"If he joins them." I say. "Maybe he sent them here so he could get some sleep."

Connie looks at me, horrified. "That's an awful thought. Why do you think such awful things, Sage?"

"It was a joke, geeze, you're no fun tonight. I'm not sure why I gave up my beauty sleep to help you out."

Connie shakes her head. We're still gazing up at the window.

The woman notices us, and her mouth is set in alarm until she recognises Connie, at which point she grins, waves, and gestures for her to wait a moment.

"She's coming down. Probably wonders why you're

wandering the streets alone at night with a hammer." I say, because Adele won't be able to see me.

Connie looks down at the hammer in her hand and hides it away in the backpack she brought out with her, which she places on the sidewalk behind the picket fence. "Good point."

"Look, I'm gonna get going back. You'll be okay?"

"Sure." Connie says. "You don't have to go, though. I'm sure she's only popping down to say hi."

"Okay." I say. I don't want to let her walk home alone.

There's a dark presence in Mystic Springs. A presence she hasn't trained her empath skills enough to pick up on yet, and one I hope I never have to protect her from.

The front door of the house opens and the blond woman appears, her feet bare, the baby swaddled into her dressing gown.

"Connie?" She calls, standing on the veranda and peering out into the darkness. "Are you okay? What are you doing out at this time?"

"Oh, I'm fine." She says. "I struggle to sleep sometimes. It's so peaceful out at this time, I thought I'd have a little walk."

"You're sure you're okay?"

"Honestly, I'm fine. I didn't mean to alarm you. I didn't even know this was your house, I just saw the light go on and looked up without thinking. You settling in okay?"

Adele laughs. She's adorable, I decide right away. The kind of woman I'd be drawn to as a friend. "The place is a tip, but I've found the coffee machine so I could care less."

"You're awfully jolly for the middle of the night, is that your secret?" Connie jokes.

"I'll crash tomorrow, don't worry. In fact, if you're free, I'll probably take a stroll to the coffee house at some point."

"That'd be great." Connie says. "Drop me a message."

"Ok, will do. Well, good night!"

"Good night Adele." Connie calls.

"I love her." I declare.

"She's pretty cool, isn't she?" Connie says.

"Did you say something?" Adele calls from the doorstep.

Connie laughs. "Nope, just thought I was going to sneeze!"

I wait until Adele returns into her home and closes the door then begin to laugh. "Look at you, making friends."

"What does that mean?" Connie says.

"Well, it's not your best skill."

"I have friends." Connie protests.

"You have clients. And neighbours."

Connie stops in her tracks. "Oh my God. You're right."

I shrug. "It's not a big deal. Geeze, I thought you knew. You just don't really get that close to people."

"I probably spend too much time with the dead." Connie quips.

"Well, don't get any ideas. I'm not going anywhere. Nobody fights with me the way you do, sis."

Connie shakes her head. "And nobody holds flyers up with the flair you do."

We laugh and then Connie gasps.

"What's up?"

"I've left the backpack. I need to go and get it."

I groan. My body aches with tiredness.

"You go on, I'll only be two minutes. I'll see you at home."

"Are you sure?" I ask, but I'm already floating away from her towards the house.

"Yes, I'll be fine. Go on." She says.

And I do.

16

CONNIE

I reflect on Sage's words as I retrace my footsteps back to Adele's house. The bedroom light is still on and I see her, standing with her back to the window, a small face peeking over her shoulder as she rocks the baby back to sleep.

I know I shouldn't, but I stand and watch. Imagine. Dream.

I always wanted children but it seems they didn't want me. I've made my peace with that mainly, but something about the intimacy of the new mother rocking her baby captivates me. It feels like the biggest event happening in the world at this moment. Why isn't the whole town out here with me, watching? How can people sleep through this?

Adele turns a fraction, plants a kiss on the baby's head, and I dive for the ground and hope she hasn't seen me.

When I peer at the house again, the lights are out.

The show's over.

I reach across the sidewalk for the backpack, but it's gone.

I let out a small, nervous laugh.

Of course it hasn't gone.

But it's gone.

I clamber to my feet and turn in a full circle. The backpack is nowhere in sight.

"Hello?" I call out, which is a ridiculous thing to do, because there's nobody there and nowhere to hide.

I shake my head. I must have misremembered where I left the bag. I'll go home and worry about it after a good night's sleep.

I ignore the churning in my stomach and begin the walk back towards my house.

I force myself to count the steps I take as I walk, but my mind fights against me, imagining noises. A twig snapping. Footsteps behind me.

When I turn, there's nobody in sight.

And yet, I'm not alone.

I pick up the pace and curse myself for not being more fit. The yoga pants I'm straining into have rarely been worn, and definitely never for yoga. I can feel a tightening in my chest, my body warning me to slow down. I've already done a full lap of the town putting up the flyers, that's more exercise than I have in a day and now I'm trying to go faster instead of collapse on the settee with a bowl of pretzels? My body says hell no.

I take a deep breath, try to steady my breathing.

I can almost see my house. Just a few more minutes.

And then I feel it. An energy so dark I find myself bursting into a run.

If I thought Devin emitted an energy I wanted to get away from, this is a hundred times worse. Just to be near it makes me cry because I know I'm not fast enough to get away.

And not strong enough to fight it.

I run as fast as I can, barely faster than the walk, and the dark energy around me is so strong I can almost see it, as a black swirling cloud around me, surrounding me, suffocating me, swallowing me whole.

"Help!" I scream, although my body can't handle the strain of running and shouting, and I have no idea if a word actually comes out.

My heartbeat hammers in my ears, blocking out all other sound. Surely, help will come when they all hear my heartbeat? Surely, someone will help me.

"Help!" I try again.

The black energy grows thicker, taking over my vision until I can no longer see the road. The world is darkness, and I have no idea which way to move or how to lift one foot after the other. I'm moving, but I can't tell which direction I'm headed in. Every step feels as though I could be plummeting to the ground.

"Please!" I scream at the top of my voice now, utterly desperate. "Help me please!"

I force myself to raise my arms, through the darkness, and rub at my eyes, hoping the world will be revealed to me again. Nothing. The world is so dark now I don't know if I'm seeing blackness or nothing, or are the two the same?

I begin to cry, and the effort of that together with the movement, is too much. I slow, and as I do, I feel a sudden crack against my head, a blow that forces me to the floor and switches the whole world off.

This is it, I think.

It's time.

**

"Connie?" A voice calls through the fog of pain. I try to open my eyes but can't. I try to groan, to make some kind of response, but I have no idea if they can hear me.

I return to sleep, to sweet dreams of bouncing babies, until the babies glare at me and pick up tiny hammers and begin to chase me. I sit up then, eyes forced open, and have no idea where I am.

"Connie, it's Adele. Can you hear me?" The attorney sits at my side. I'm in a hospital bed, hooked up to a machine that beeps rhythmically. The room is bright lights and bleach and I love it. I want to live here, in a world so artificially lit that the darkness can never return.

"Do you remember who did this to you?" She asks. She is baby-free and this troubles me.

"Where... where are... babies?" I manage. My throat feels like a desert.

"Oh." Adele laughs. "My husband's joined us now. Don't worry about them. Do you remember what happened?"

I try to shake my head, stop when shooting pain spasms across me.

"Someone attacked you." Adele says. "With a hammer. You didn't see who it was?"

"No." I admit. I could have turned around. I could have looked behind me, but I was too scared. I didn't want to know.

"Well, don't worry. They'll catch whoever it was."

"They?"

"The police."

"We have no police." I say. That's the only reason I was out at that time of night flyering to catch a murderer.

"Oh, didn't I say? My husband's the new Sheriff."

**

Taylor Morton is an English gentleman, impressive in his uniform, generous in his attentions.

He insists on paying for a private ambulance to drive me home when I get the all clear, and then he paces around my old house checking that every lock is secure and every window fitting is in place. He draws curtains, tests smoke alarms, and removes anything that could be considered a weapon from the garden.

It's clear that Taylor Morton believes my life is in danger.

"He's a planner." Adele says. She sits with me in the lounge, mindlessly pushing the stroller back and forth to keep both babies asleep. The miracle she has been dreaming of, and she's stuck here looking after me instead of enjoying the peace. "He means well, but he can be a bit over the top with it all."

I nod my head and immediately wish I hadn't. Pain shoots across my temple.

I hear Taylor stride back towards us. He appears in the doorway, bald head gleaming, dark rimmed spectacles sitting on his slim nose. He looks too bookish to be a Sheriff, and yet as soon as he moves, or speaks, it's clear he's a man in control.

"I still think you should come stay with us, ma'am." He says, not a hint of the British accent left. He moved to the US when he was 10, Adele has explained, and now he feels about as American as apple pie.

"Honestly, I'll be fine." I say. "I have plenty to be getting on with."

"Like what?" He asks.

"Well... my work."

"What do you do for work exactly?"

"I'm a medium." I say. This is always an awkward moment. Depending on who I tell, I either go up or down in their estimation when they hear this.

"I see." He says. His reaction is impossible to read. He must be used to people much more strange than me.

"Oh, I didn't realise." Adele gushes by my side. "I've always wanted to see a medium. Do you, like... read fortunes and things?"

"No." I say. It's a common misunderstanding. I have no more idea what a strong love line looks like than how to prepare for a marathon. "That's something different. If you've lost someone, I can sometimes contact that spirit and allow you to speak to each other through me."

"Oh, that's wonderful." She says. "That must be so nice for people."

"I think so." I say. It isn't always wonderful, though. Sometimes the spirits don't say what people want to hear. Death does not heal all tensions, lemme tell ya.

"Well." Taylor says, then coughs. "You live alone?"

I nod. "I mean, my sister's here most of the time. But she's a spirit."

"Could she protect you?" He asks. If he's cynical, he's professional enough not to show it. Or maybe he thinks it's the head injury.

I shake my head and wince. "Spirits can't hurt people."

"So effectively, you're here alone. Do you realise that someone tried to kill you, Connie?"

"Well... I..." I say, and feel my throat constrict as tears build up. "I wouldn't want to put it exactly like that."

"That's exactly what happened, there's no reason to put

it any other way. Someone out there tried to kill you. Someone's already killed Lola Anti. Now, I'm going to investigate these things, but my priority is keeping you safe. Will you please come and stay with us?"

"No." I say, remembering not to move my head. "I can't. I have to be here. I'll be careful, I promise."

Taylor sighs and shrugs. He glances across at Adele but her gaze is focused on the babies in the stroller.

"And anyway, if I'm in your home, I'm putting your children at risk." I say, sure that I've just found my trump card.

"Not really." Taylor says. "Whoever did this was coming after you. Nobody else."

His words send a shiver down my spine and for a moment I'm tempted to pack a bag and go across to his house. I can imagine a future of slotting myself onto the edge of their family. Grateful for the shelter, I'd make myself useful by getting up early and making pancakes for everyone's breakfast, then I'd offer to mind the babies so Adele could take a shower. In the afternoon we'd walk to the coffee house together, taking it in turns to push the stroller and drink our drinks as the babies woke and slept and cried and nursed. It could be a good life.

"I'll be okay." I whisper. "And, Sheriff, you should know, I've been investigating Lola's murder."

"You've what?" He asks, outraged. "Don't you see how dangerous it is? You've made yourself a target."

"With respect, I wasn't keen to get involved, trust me, but we had no law enforcement before you arrived."

"So you became the police force?"

"Me and a few spirits. The former Sheriff, Patton Davey, and a couple of others."

"Davey?"

I nod, then curse.

"I know him." Taylor says. "We trained together. I didn't know he'd passed."

"He's a good guy." I say.

"Yeah, he sure was. That's too bad. I knew he'd headed up this way, I just thought he must have moved on somewhere else."

"He has, in a way." I say with a smile. "He's still very involved. I bet he'd like to speak to you again, if you ever want me to contact him for you."

Taylor shifts from one foot to the other, his heavy-duty boots clomping as he does. "I'll give that some thought."

A baby begins to cry and Adele groans.

"You guys should get going." I say. "You've done more than enough for me. Really, I'm so grateful."

"You have a spare key?" Taylor asks.

"Mm, I think so." I say. I've never had reason to give a spare key out to anyone.

"Would you be happy to give it to me? I'd like to pop by in the night, make sure everything's okay."

"I guess." I say. "I just... if I hear someone walking around in here, how will I know if it's you or..."

"I could shout out when I come in?" He suggests.

"Surely, if you can see that the outside's secure, there's no reason to come inside and spook her?" Adele says.

Taylor cocks his head to one side. "I guess. Okay, I'll do that. I'll be over tonight to check the outside. If you need anything at all, you call me, okay? I'll keep my phone on and I'm just a minute away."

I remember how quickly the blackness swallowed me.

A minute away is too far.

17

CONNIE

*T*he pity party lasts for exactly four hours and twelve minutes.

I know because during that time I lie on the couch and watch the clock move, listening to every creak in this old house and fearing another attack.

I vow to keep my nose out of anyone else's business and, in my mind, I hang up my murder investigation hat and look forward to a quiet life, while simultaneously fearing that I don't have much life left to live at all.

And then, four hours and twelve minutes after Adele and Taylor and their beautiful babies have left, I feel a rage like I've never experienced before.

"Damn you." I mutter. I'm pacing the bedroom at this point, unable to sleep. Hyped up, full of energy, which could be the drugs the hospital gave me. "You've messed with the wrong woman."

"Hell, yeah, there she is." Sage sings out, appearing for the first time since the attack happened. She looks sheepish, but I'm not angry with her. Spirits can't hurt the living, that's a well-known fact, despite the horror film industry wanting you to believe otherwise. There was nothing she could have done. "You ready to kick some ass?"

"I'm gonna find out who did this, and who hurt Lola. It's time to step this investigation up a notch."

"Woohoo!" Sage cheers, pretending to shake pom poms in the air. She would have been a great cheerleader if we'd grown up here. Back home in England, we were both stuck with drizzly matches of hockey in the school field. Enough to put a girl off sport for life, which it did in my case.

"First stop, Nettie Frasier. Coming?" I ask.

Sage shakes her head too quick, actually floats backwards a little.

"What's wrong? You love looking in people's houses." I say. The rule here is that spirits can't let themselves into someone's home uninvited. It's our way of protecting people's privacy. My way of reassuring any locals nervous of our spirit community that they don't have to listen out for bumps in the night. I know the rule gets broken, of course, but it's frowned upon. And the spirits tend to police themselves. So for Sage to refuse an open invitation into Nettie's beautiful home, something is up.

"I don't like that house." Sage says.

"Are you kidding? It's beautiful." I argue. Desmond's investment banker money afforded the couple a home that almost rivals Violet's in terms of size and grandeur. I've never been inside it, but I know the layout. I checked out the sale listing after they'd bought it. The house is out of this world.

"There's just something... something bad there, Connie. Be careful."

I refuse to be afraid. I'm going to confront Nettie, suggest that she killed Lola as revenge for her affair with Desmond, and then hurt me to stop me investigating. It all fits together, and I've told Patton (who did his own moonlight supervision of the house to make sure I was safe) to accompany me. He won't be able to do anything to help me, if things go wrong, but I'll feel more confident with a witness.

"I'll be fine." I say, forcing a smile onto my face. "And anyway, I have a client in a couple of hours. If I'm not back then, call for help."

Sage grimaces but doesn't try to stop me.

I grab my jacket and slip into my shoes, and brave the world outside.

**

Nettie answers the door on the third ring, just as I was about to wonder if my visit will be wasted. I'm not sure I'll find the courage to return a second time and, indeed, by the time she answers the door in a cherry-patterned apron, her hair falling in perfect ringlets, I can feel my nerve already slipping away.

"Connie? Are you okay?" She asks.

I nod. "Can I come in? I need to talk to you."

"Erm." She murmurs and glances behind me, down the path, straight through Patton who will follow me in if she allows me entry. We don't have the kind of relationship where I can show up unannounced and ask to enter, and my request troubles her. "It's not really a good time."

"It's important." I say.

"Let's go to the coffee house?" She suggests. "The house is a bit of a mess."

"It needs to be here." I say. I wonder what she's hiding in this big, grand home. A home that never hosts dinners, parties, or even informal movie nights. A home that never sees guests invited over.

She looks down at the veranda and I wonder for a moment if she will just slam the door in my swollen face, but she sighs and holds the door open, stands to one side, allows me to walk in.

"We can go in the sitting room." She says, gesturing to a room off towards the left. She leads the way. The room is palatial, but nothing apart from the size is impressive. It's nothing like the photos I saw of how it looked before she moved in.

I do a full 360 and take in the whole of the room. The peeling wallpaper and the sagging couch. And then I look at Nettie, who is as immaculate as always. Outfit perfectly colour-coordinated, hair style straight from a salon, make-up applied expertly.

" I know, it's a mess." She says, clearly seeing my reaction.

"Oh, no, no. Your home is beautiful." I lie. It was beautiful, I think. From the sale photos, I know there was no work to be done. It was immaculate. How on Earth could Nettie have allowed it to end up like this?

She laughs. "It's a complete mess. That's why I didn't want you to come in. I'm working on it, but things break quicker than I can mend them, ya know?"

"Oh yeah." I agree, but I don't know. Wallpaper manages to stay up on the walls in my house.

"Drink?" She offers.

"Sure." I say. I'm completely thrown off-course by the state of the house and have no idea how I plan on accusing her of being a murderer. I need to buy time. "You have any sweet tea?"

"Mm-hmm, I think I do. I won't be a moment." Nettie

says. She leaves the room and I exchange glances with Patton, who floats near the window, and then take the chance to explore the room in more detail. The wall is black around the power socket, as if the electricity has blown.

A small bang erupts from the kitchen and I jump and move out of sight.

"Damn it!" Nettie exclaims.

I go to her, ignoring the threadbare rug over the hardwood floor. I recognise the kitchen from the show photos. The room is circular, with a round island in the middle, large windows, and French doors leading out into the garden. It's a complete, and utter, mess.

Dirty dishes are piled on the granite countertops, a pile of soggy laundry sits on the floor, and Nettie stands, head in her hands, in front of a kettle as black smoke pours out of it.

"Are you okay?" I ask.

Nettie shakes her head and refuses to look at me. "Can you just go? I don't want you to see me like this."

"I'm not going anywhere." I say. "We need to talk. You know that, right?"

She looks at me then, eyes wide. I can't picture her stabbing a young woman to death, but then I can't imagine discovering a husband's affair and not wanting to kill him and the mistress.

"Everything in this house is falling apart." She says quietly. "The kettle was fine this morning. I sat here and had a cup of tea. And now, look at it! I can't take much more of this."

"You can replace it." I try to soothe her, needing to keep the conversation focused.

"And the dishwasher? And the washer?" She asks with a groan. "I can't replace them as quick as they break."

"Nettie, please. I need to talk to you."

She takes a deep breath and pulls out a stool from the island, slumps down onto it. I stay standing. Patton hovers near the doorway.

"We have a new Sheriff in town." I say. "He's going to be investigating Lola's murder. And the attempted murder against me."

Nettie blinks. "The what against you?"

"Attempted murder." I say.

She looks downward, curls spilling across her face as a shield. "Someone tried to hurt you?"

"Someone did hurt me." I correct. "Last night. I was lucky to survive."

Nettie returns her gaze to me, then takes a deep, pained breath and closes her eyes. "I'm so sorry."

"Do you know anything about it?" I ask.

She shakes her head, darts a glance across towards me.

"Are you sure? Because the obvious thing to think is that it's connected with Lola's murder. That the killer was trying to stop me discovering who they were."

"Why would *you* discover who they were?" She asks, and her question jolts me.

Of course. If I'm a target because of the investigation, the only possible suspects are people who know about the investigation.

"I don't know." I lie, no longer sure who to trust and who not to trust. "I'm just trying to talk to everyone. I need to know who did this to me."

"Of course." Nettie says. She glances around the room. "It's an awful feeling, that someone is trying to hurt you."

"Just out of interest, were you at the party?"

"The April Fools' Party?" Nettie asks. "No. I knew she'd be there. I didn't want to see her."

"Lola?"

She nods and a single tear falls, cutting a line through her make-up, revealing a slice of natural skin tone there's no reason for her to hide. "Desmond and I didn't have the perfect marriage, especially towards the end. You could say I hated him for what he did. We were so young when we met. I knew I was beautiful back then. I was that kind of cheer-leader girl, perfect tan girl, ride in the back of your truck girl. I never realised my legs would start to wobble. I thought wrinkles were for other people. I wasn't ready to age but, more than that, Desmond wasn't ready for me to age. And as soon as I did, he looked elsewhere. I knew it was happening, I'm not stupid. But I thought, maybe, if I could be perfect enough, maybe he'd stop. Maybe I'd be enough."

I bite my lip. "He was a damn fool, girl."

She laughs, my bluntness cutting through the emotion. "Oh, I know that now. I realised it, just too late. He and Lola, they deserved each other. She was playing him just like he was using her. As soon as she got too needy, or her body started to sag a little, he'd be on to the next one. What a sad way to live."

"Are you okay living in this place alone?" I ask.

She looks at me then, a steely determination in her eyes. "Oh yes. This is my home. I'm going nowhere."

CONNIE

"*Y*ou're wanted." I call out into the empty house. "Patton?"

Silence.

I hope he shows up. He disappeared pretty quick after we left Nettie.

No time to worry, though, as the doorbell rings.

I smooth down the orange and purple dress I'm wearing and pull it open, determined to offer my biggest smile.

"You could have just let yourself in." I say with a laugh.

Taylor Morton smiles at me and holds my spare key out for me. "I wouldn't do that. You want it back? Everything seemed fine last night but I was ready to come in if needed."

"Everything's fine." I say. "Come on in."

He's already been here, of course, but he was here last night as my caregiver, my protector. The Sheriff. Today, he's here as a client, and I want to impress him with my professionalism. I'm still convinced he's only here at Adele's insistence. I can imagine her, behind the scenes, suggesting he take me up on my offer and make an appointment. Plus it allows him to unofficially check on my welfare.

I show him through to the consultation room, where I've already put out two glasses of water and opened a window. The air was a little stale in the room, it's freshened up now.

"So, how does this work?" He asks. "I've never done this before."

"I'll invite the spirit in and then you can just say whatever you want out loud, and I'll tell you what they say in response. I can't guarantee they'll turn up, but like I say, Patton is still pretty involved, so it shouldn't be an issue."

"I don't want to speak to Patton." Taylor says with a nervous smile.

"Oh. Okay. I just..."

"I mean, I might want to speak to him another time. But for now, I want to speak to someone else. Ya know, if that's possible."

"I usually ask for an item that belongs to the person. I guess you don't have anything?" I say.

"I do." He says. He reaches into his pocket and pulls out a delicate, silver anklet, which he passes across to me. I clasp it in my hands and close my eyes, a whirlwind of emotions hitting my senses as I focus only on the jewelry.

"Lola." I say. Her face comes clearly into view in my mind, her bee-stung lips, thick eyebrows, tousled hair, attitude. I open my eyes. "You knew her?"

He shakes his head. "I picked this up from the evidence container across town. My wife told me you'd need something."

"I have to warn you, I doubt this will work." I say with a sigh. "Someone's already tried to reach her."

"We can try." He says, and takes a long sip of water.

"Okay. Lola Anti, if you can hear me, I have the new Sheriff here. We'd like very much to speak to you. We wish you only well. If you can hear me, please make yourself known. We want to help you."

Silence.

I take a sip of water too, to give me something to do as we wait.

"Is it common for spirits not to, erm, tune in? Or whatever you'd call it." Taylor asks.

"Not for me, no." I say. "They usually respond. But it's their choice."

"It's a lovely house you have here." Taylor says, his eyes taking in the room. "I thought it last night but it didn't seem the time to mention it."

"Thank you, for last night. I can't remember if I said it already."

"Only about a hundred times." He says with a grin. "It's fine. And anyway, I owe you. My wife told me about your kindness, holding the babies so she could have a hot drink. She was pretty down before then, you know."

"Really?"

"Yeah, this whole thing's been awful timing. Moving so soon after the babies arrived. We should have all moved at the same time, but I had a big case I needed to finish in the city, and by that point the movers had got all our furniture, the new people were ready to move into our house. It seemed like me staying behind on my own was the best thing, but I don't know. I was worried about Adele." He says, then notices the concern in my eyes. "Oh, nothing serious. She was just lonely. And she's given up a pretty big career to stay home, that's why I took the transfer, we can live on my wage here. So I was pretty psyched when I heard she'd made a friend."

I beam at his words. "I really didn't do anything more than cuddle a cute baby for a while. Trust me, most people here would jump at that chance if they had it. Your wife won't have any shortage of people to love on those babies."

He laughs. "That's good. They say it takes a village to raise a child, so it must need a whole town to raise twins."

I smile, but don't want to lose the focus of the meeting. "Lola, if you are out there, please know that this is a safe space for you. We are here wanting to speak to you. Please join us."

"I gather she wasn't this shy when alive?" Taylor asks, and something about his tone tells me he doesn't believe. He's here to check on me, without making it appear that way. I try not to be insulted.

And then, in a manifestation so sudden and powerful the window slams shut, she arrives.

Sultry and simmering, as powerful in death as she was alive, she remains by the window, glaring at me and Taylor, who has spilt his glass of water all over his khaki slacks.

"Lola. This is Taylor Morton, he's the new Sheriff. He's going to find out who did this to you, and he's going to have them punished. Will you help him?"

Lola moves across the room, taking a close look at the Sheriff. She says nothing. I gesture towards Taylor to be quiet, and sit back in my chair, giving her the time she needs.

"You want my help?" She asks, finally.

"We want your help. Taylor, why don't you tell Lola how she could help you with the investigation."

Taylor clears his throat. His skin has blanched and his right leg shakes involuntarily. "Lola, hello. I want to find the person who did this to you. Do you know who that was? I can have them arrested and sent to a grand jury."

Lola laughs. "I'm sure they'll be terrified."

"Lola." I say. "Help us."

She rolls her eyes. "Have you spoken to Nettie? You know she's the obvious one, right? I mean, she did assault me. I guess she couldn't handle her husband finding a younger model."

"Did she do it?" I ask, then turn to Taylor who is watching the one-sided conversation in confusion. "She's asking if you've spoken to Nettie. Nettie Frasier."

"I haven't spoken to anyone yet." Taylor says. "I like to speak to the victim first, if possible."

Good policy, I think, but he's never spoken to a murder victim before. And this victim isn't all innocent herself.

"Did Nettie do it?" I repeat.

Lola approaches Taylor, until she is almost touching his face with her own. She flutters her eyelashes at him, pouts her lips. He shivers.

"He's not bad." Lola says. "And a wife with two new babies. He must be in the market himself for a younger model. Shame I can't fill the vacancy..."

"Lola, try and pay attention. We're trying to help you." I scold. She's infuriating.

"Geeze, can't a spirit have a little fun now and then? You really should lighten up. Now, where were we? Nettie, Nettie, Nettie. The grieving widow. Isn't it a coincidence, both her husband and his mistress dead."

I sigh. "She isn't being very helpful, Sheriff."

"That's okay." He says. "She's been through a lot. She probably doesn't know who to trust. Lola, if you're listening to me, I promise I only want to help you. I want to help you because you didn't deserve to be hurt. But also because you didn't deserve to be used the way you were when you were alive. You should have been treated better."

His words stop her in her tracks. "What does he mean?"

"She asks what you mean by that."

"I know what happened to you." He says. "I know what you were running from."

Lola clenches her hands into fists. "Tell him to shut up. He doesn't know what he's talking about."

"I know you were running from a man who promised to protect you. He wore my uniform, didn't he? That's why I'm here in my casual clothes. I'm not like that man. I promise you, Lola, I want nothing from you. And I know you're not used to that."

"He needs to stop talking." Lola says, agitated. She glares at Taylor. I feel my heart pounding in my chest.

"She's asking you to stop talking." I say.

"I'm not going to." Taylor says. "You have nothing to hide, Lola. Nothing to be ashamed of. That man was no Sheriff. That uniform wasn't real. He was a criminal and a bully, and he made you promises he couldn't keep. He told you he'd keep you safe, didn't he? From the boyfriend who'd been beating you."

"Shut up!" She screams, and Taylor flinches. He can't hear her but he senses her energy, I realise.

"It started with small things, didn't it? Stealing small things. Selling little bags of powder. You knew it was wrong but he was the only one who'd looked after you. If he said it was okay, you trusted him. But then you started to see another side to him. He let his guard down, let the mask slip. A slap, a kick... a trip to the hospital. He wasn't protecting you, but you were stuck, weren't you?"

"He needs to stop." Lola says, and this time, her voice is cracked, through tears.

"His name was James Thompson. And you weren't the first girl he treated that way, or the last. But it's finished now. I built a case against him, just like I'll build a case against

whoever took your life. He's not going to hurt anyone else."
Taylor says, his own eyes wet with tears.

I gulp. "Lola, can you give us some information about
who hurt you?"

She lets out a bitter sneer. "Everyone in my damn life
hurt me. Take your pick. They can all rot in Hell."

"We're here to help you." I say, trying to soothe her, to
reach the girl she must have been before she entered a
world of manipulation, crime and fear. "Please let us
help you."

"You want to help me?" She asks, and she dries her tears
and moves across towards Taylor again. Her bravado has
gone, and in its place is pure anger. "You? You want to
help me?"

"Yes, we want to help you." I say.

"Lola, I won't rest until the person who hurt you is
locked away. They will be punished for what they did to
you. You can trust me. I will make sure they're caught, and
punished."

"You have no idea." She says with a sad smile, and then
she pulls her arm back, clenches her fist, and shoots
forward, her fist connecting with Taylor's jaw. The blow
knocks him into the back of the chair. A single tooth rolls
out from his mouth as he grips his face. Blood drips onto
the couch.

And that is how I realise.

Spirits can harm the living, after all.

19

SAGE

I insist on going with Connie as she walks Taylor Morton back to his house, because frankly this town is becoming crazy and I don't want my sister out of my sight any more. I float along and try to stay tuned in to the energy around us, but the Sheriff is a steaming pile of anger and humiliation and I'm a little worried I'll miss anything else that might be out there.

"I wish you'd let me take you to hospital." Connie says, for the millionth time.

Taylor shakes his head. He has a wad of tissue paper in his hand but the bleeding has mainly stopped. His lost tooth has been cleaned by my industrious sister and is in his pocket. Lord knows why he wants to keep it, but he does. Probably so used to gathering evidence he can't help himself.

"This has never happened before." Connie says, also for the millionth time. She talks too much when she's nervous. "I'm mortified. I mean, Lola had such an attitude, but she was never violent. And everyone knows spirits can't hurt humans."

"Clearly." I mutter.

Connie shoots me a glare.

"Look, I'll take it from here." Taylor says. "I'll be fine, honestly. I was provoking her and I got what I deserved. I just thought if I could cut through the tough-guy act, she might work with us more. I need to explain this to Adele on my own. I'm still going to keep an eye on your place, okay? You need to be cautious still."

"Okay." Connie agrees. "If you're sure."

"Absolutely." Taylor says. He walks ahead and we turn to head back towards home.

"I prefer Patton." I say.

"Sage, are you serious? How can you think about that kind of stuff at a time like this?"

I shrug. "I like to try and find the light-hearted pleasures in life."

"You like to find the fine men in life."

"Or in death." I quip, and a small smile passes across her lips.

"I can't believe a spirit has hurt a living person." Connie says. "This is huge news. We need to tell Patton."

"It is a little worrying." I admit.

"It's terrifying." Connie says.

"And she didn't give any suggestion of who killed her?"

Connie sighs. "She just kept mentioning Nettie. But not saying she'd actually done it. And Nettie says she wasn't even at the party. Do you remember her being there?"

"Nope." I say. "And I was looking. I knew there'd be some big ass drama if they were both there together. I didn't see her."

"Hmm." Connie murmurs. "I don't buy it. I don't think it's her. It's too obvious."

"So who does that leave us with? As suspects?" I wonder

aloud. "Atticus is determined it's Desiree, but she wasn't in town. Violet was practically begging to be a suspect."

"What about the supermodel?" Connie says.

"Devin Summer? No way."

"Why? Because she's famous and beautiful?" Connie scoffs.

"Well, yeah." I say. They sound like as good a reason as any other in this crazy case so far.

"She's got such a dark energy." Connie says. "And whoever hurt me, they had that energy."

I shrug. "I think she's just one of those moody artistic people."

"Ugh, modelling is not art!" Connie exclaims. "It's pure vanity. And vanity for people who are a size zero. I hate the whole industry."

"Okay then." I say, eyes wide, unsure where her outrage has come from. "Don't shoot the messenger, it's not my fault that I happen to be beautiful and a size zero."

"You died when you were young enough to still be a size zero." Connie says, which is just mean, and blatantly untrue. She's never been a size zero in her life. Clearly, we're getting nowhere discussing this together.

"Let's talk it all through in the next meeting." I say.

Connie sighs as we approach the Frasier house. "There's something strange going on in there."

"I did tell you that." I say, trying not to gloat too much.

"It's like the house is working against her." Connie says.

"Well, anything's possible." I say. I'm distracted. Tonight, I get to visit Rydell Grove's police station with Patton. It is absolutely not a first date. But still. It's the closest I've come to a first date in a good two decades and I plan to be entertaining, adorable, breathtakingly attractive, and, of course, incredibly professional.

Tonight, I feel, may be the night that Patton falls head over heels for me.

Not that I'm on the market. I'm officially married, although one lifetime was long enough with that man, thank you very much. No, I don't want to hook up, but I'd quite like an admirer. Someone who looks at me the way Adele Morton looks at those plump little babies. Wait. Is that weird?

"Earth calling Sage." Connie calls to me.

"Huh?" I ask.

"I said, what's she doing." Connie repeats, gesturing to Nettie's front lawn, where Nettie stands, staring into space.

"I have no idea, but it's nothing to do with us." I say, because I know how my sister's mind works. She wants us to go over there. And there's no way I'm doing that.

"We need to check she's okay." Connie says.

"No we don't." I say. "There's every chance she killed Lola and tried to kill you. I'm not letting you go across there. Let's just tell Patton, or Taylor. Let them deal with it."

"Fine." Connie says, and as we cross the street away from the house, I watch Nettie walk towards the metal bin at the side of the house, lift the lid, and toss something inside.

"Did you see that?" I ask.

Connie nods. "One of us can come out later and take a look."

"Not one of us." I correct. "This is over our heads now, one of the Sheriffs can pick up this lead."

"You know what? Let's find Patton and see if he can look now."

I nod my agreement. If I argue it, she'll only be tempted to go across on her own.

**

We find Patton in Connie's attic, which she is not happy about. She spends a good two minutes muttering under her breath about privacy and nobody respecting laws anymore, which is a little ironic in front of the Sheriff.

"So. Taylor Morton?" Patton says, and it's me he directs the question at.

I flutter my eyelashes just a little, going for effortless beauty rather than full-on flirt. "The Sheriff? I think that's his name."

"I know damn well that's his name. I can't believe his cheek."

"He said he knew you." Connie says.

Patton smirks. "You could say we have some history."

"Ooh, is there drama here, Sheriff?" I ask. "I told my sister you're clearly the better Sheriff by miles, by the way."

Patton rolls his eyes.

"Can we stay focused?" Connie barks. "Patton, something major's happened. Lola Anti hit Taylor Morton today. I saw it with my own eyes."

I expect Patton to laugh at the thought of his arch-rival being attacked, but he gasps. Actually gasps. "She hit him?"

Connie nods. "Connected with him. Drew blood. Have you ever heard of that happening before?"

"Never." Patton says. "It doesn't happen. It can't. Except, clearly it can."

"And there's more. We've just seen Nettie Frasier acting strange, and then she hid something in her garbage. I think we should go and check it out."

"Let's go." Patton says, springing into action. He's like a

coiled spring, ready to move into action with a moment's notice.

Connie turns to me. "You're coming."

I sigh and follow them out of the house and across the street. Nettie's lawn is empty, her front door is closed. Her car isn't on the drive.

"She's gone out." Connie says, reading my thoughts.

"Okay, what did you see exactly?" Patton asks.

"It was over here." Connie says, leading the way. I hang back, by the picket fence. She strides across the lawn to the garbage bin, Patton floating at her heels. "She was just staring into space, as if she was in shock or something. And then she came across here, and lifted the lid, and -"

"Stop." Patton says as Connie reaches out for the garbage bin. "Don't touch it, you'll leave prints. Let me."

The whirr of a car approaching makes the hairs on the back of my neck stand to attention. I glance down the road, see the vehicle I know getting closer. "Guys, we have company."

"We only need a second." Connie calls to me as Nettie's vehicle approaches.

Patton lifts the garbage lid and begins to rifle through Nettie's laundry.

Nettie pulls in to the driveway and notices my sister at the side of her home. "Connie? What are you doing?"

I take a deep breath and edge onto the lawn. I have no idea what help I will be, but I know I can't do anything hiding out by the fence.

Connie spins on her heels and offers Nettie a smile. "I thought I smelt something..."

I groan. She's always been an awful liar.

"I'm calling the police." Nettie says. "This is getting out of hand, your interest in me."

She stalks back across to the house, gives Connie one last withering look, slams the door behind her.

"I've got it." Patton says, and he emerges from the bin. At first I don't see the blade, but when I do, I feel as if I may faint.

She did it, she did it, she did it.

"Connie." I warn.

"Oh God." She murmurs.

I focus on the lush green grass, the chipped wood of the veranda, the glow of perspiration on my sister's face. Anything but that weapon.

"It's still got blood on it." Patton says. "As much as I hate the man, we need to get Taylor across here so he can bag it and tag it."

"I'll fetch him." Connie says, and takes off towards the Sheriff's house in her idea of a run.

I float awkwardly on the veranda, watching as the blinds twitch and Nettie peers out. She watches Connie leave and, for a moment, looks right at me. Or right through me. She shows no sign of being able to see me. It's the strangest sensation, seeing but being unseen.

Taylor appears just seconds later, his boots clonking on the sidewalk as he comes running into sight. Patton lays the knife back in the garbage and stands aside as the new Sheriff approaches, spots it, and takes out his cell.

"I'm bringing in a suspected murder weapon, have the lab open and ready." He says, authoritative.

The front door opens. "What the hell is going on here?"

Taylor and Patton both turn and eye up Nettie, scouring her body for concealed weapons, assessing the threat this immaculate woman may present to them. Their training transforms them into mirror images of the other.

"Nettie Frasier." Taylor says. "You're under arrest on

suspicion of the murder of Lola Anti and the attempted murder of Connie Winters. You have the right to remain silent. Anything you say can and will be used against you in a court of law. You have the right to have an attorney. If you cannot afford one, one will be appointed to you by the court. I'll require you to come with me now, ma'am."

"Wait." Connie calls, as she reaches the picket fence. Her face is beet red and the baby hairs around her forehead lay flat against her skin, glued to her by the sweat that covers her face and leaves damp patches across her body. She grabs on to the gate and bends over, gasping for her next breath.

"Are you okay?" I call. I've never seen her like this.

She nods, gasps, then returns to a standing position. Taylor is manhandling Nettie into a hold.

"Wait, Sheriff." Connie repeats. "She's being set up."

20

CONNIE

*A*ll of the eyes are on me, and it's pretty disconcerting. I've just ran further than I have since upper school, when the awfully named Mr Chicken had taunted me with cries of *put some effort in* and *you run like a wet lettuce* while I legitimately confronted my fear of death and gave in to what I was certain must be a heart attack.

I hadn't died then, clearly, but I always felt I'd skimmed death with a proximity I didn't want to repeat. And so, my running career was declared over on that day. For the remaining PE lessons before I was able to leave with flying colours in every single subject except, you guessed it, PE, I faked sick notes. It was the height of my rule breaking and I didn't even feel shame.

And yet here I find myself, years later and a couple of stones heavier (okay, more than a couple), struggling to breathe, droplets of salty sweat dripping into my open mouth, and the people gathered around watching me appear entirely unimpressed.

I ran here, you buffoons is what I'd like to say, as they stand around and wait for me to explain more.

Nettie stands in a bizarre position, restrained by Sheriff Morton who isn't quite ready to let go of her yet even though he isn't in uniform and has nowhere to take her. There's no squad car to pile her into. What does he plan on doing? Walking her across town to the nearest jail?

I collapse to the ground and focus on my breathing, which refuses to steady.

This could be it. The end of the road.

I wonder if Mr Chicken is alive and what he'd make of news of my sport-related death. He'd probably forgotten my name before I'd made it off school premises that final time.

Not one of the pretty girls who hung around the football pitch pretending not to be interested in matches the popular boys played, and not one of the sporty girls who brought home medals for him to display in the wall cabinets for hockey or rounders or netball or, well, anything more exerting than algebra. I was of no interest to him.

"You must be able to breathe now?" Sage asks, and if I had the energy I'd be tempted to see if the living can hurt spirits, since I now know it works the other way around. My sister. Adorable in a completely infuriating way.

I take a final shaky breath and then attempt to climb to my feet, but I feel a twinge in the back of my leg and collapse back down to the ground. They can come to me.

And they do.

Sheriff Morton leads Nettie as gently as he can, while continuing to restrain her, and my sister and Patton bring up the rear.

"You think she's being set up?" Sheriff Morton asks, looking at me from above his spectacles, which have dropped down his nose as he looks down at me.

I nod. "It's the murder weapon, isn't it?"

Sheriff Morton glances at Nettie, then back to me. "This is police business now..."

"Oh, please. I know what's happening. You've found the murder weapon in her garbage. I realised after I fetched you – there's no way the murderer would stand on her lawn gazing at the murder weapon before dumping it in her own bin."

"But that's what happened."

"Yes, everything except she isn't the murderer. I think the real killer planted it, probably somewhere obvious, for her to find, which she had just done when Sage and I walked past. She panicked and hid it in the closest place she could."

"It was in the flower bed." Nettie says, nodding her pretty little head.

"You'd been hiding the weapon in the flower bed?" Sheriff Morton asks.

"Geeze, he's even slower than I remember him being." Patton murmurs. Sage gushes at his side.

"No." Nettie says. "I found it in my flower bed today. It wasn't even hidden. And it definitely wasn't there yesterday."

"How can you be sure?"

"I'm out here every day. Gardening is what I do. It helps me relax." Nettie explains. "If this knife had been in my garden, I'd have seen it right away. Whoever put it there, they did it today. And if I hadn't come out here quickly and seen it, someone else would have."

"So, you find a knife in your lawn. Did you realise it was the murder weapon?"

"I thought that was a sensible conclusion to draw." Nettie says.

"You called the police, I'm guessing? Over in Rydell or Jefferson?"

Nettie shakes her head. "I hid it and then went for a drive. I needed to think. I didn't know what to do."

"And then you came home."

"And saw Connie." Nettie continues. She looks at me and I wish I could scoop her up in a hug. Who could want to inflict more pain on this woman who's already suffered so much pain and humiliation? "I knew she'd found it, I'm not stupid. I just wasn't ready to deal with it. I know I should have called the police, I do know that. And I would have. I was just nervous."

"I'll still need to take you into the station for questioning, you know that right?" Sheriff Morton says, but he releases her from his grip. Nettie nods her head then stretches her arms out behind her back.

"Do you know who might want to frame you?" I ask her.

"Well, the killer, I guess." Nettie says with a shrug. "But I don't know who that could be. From what I can gather, Lola didn't have any friends around here."

"Erm, Connie." Sage says, her gaze focused on the house. "You might want to tell Nettie that there's smoke coming from her house."

Sure enough, a plume of thick smoke appears from the open front door.

"Nettie..." I begin, and she sees the alarm on my face and turns to look at the destruction being caused.

She lets out a groan and drops to her knees on the lawn. "Damn it."

Sheriff Morton dives across the lawn, onto the veranda and then pushes the door open. "It's okay, it's just a waste paper basket that's caught fire. Right by the door, it looks worse than it is. Were you trying to burn things, Mrs Frasier?"

Nettie lets out a bitter laugh. "Yes, I was. My marriage papers. Not worth the paper they're printed on."

"Some people might say it's suspicious having a fire right around the time you find evidence to implicate you in a murder."

"Why, Sheriff?" Nettie asks, and even as she addresses the official, her poise is perfect, posture elegant. "Because clearly I'd kept a diary about it all that I realised I needed to burn?"

Taylor Morton allows a small smile at her retort. "Why now, ma'am?"

Nettie sighs. "Because I received a letter today. I've been receiving them every few days, letters from Lola. Detailing her affair with my husband. Every last detail. I've burnt every one when it arrived. After reading them, of course, I'm not smart enough to leave them unread. And today, I decided to burn all of the papers that ever bound me to that man. Wedding photos too. I wanted rid of it all."

"Lola Anti had been writing to you?" Sheriff Morton asks, and I see his mind whirring. Sure, I think she is being set up, but to his logical brain, she still has the biggest motive to want Lola dead. And she just made her motive even bigger.

Nettie swallows and licks her lips. "I didn't kill her, Sheriff. I have too much to lose."

The sheriff raises an eyebrow. "Like what?"

"All this." She says, gesturing with her arms around the land her property sits on. "It's gone in an instant if I take up a life of crime."

"I'm pretty sure our administration doesn't take your property just like that." Sheriff Morton says with a shake of his head. "Nice story, though. Now, let's move things along. We need to get going."

"I'll come with you." I say. "Help restrain the prisoner and all that. I'm guessing you need to walk her back to yours?"

"Fine." Taylor says. The three of us begin the walk towards the sheriff's house, and when he piles Nettie into the back of his regular vehicle and then drives off with her, I turn and walk down his path, and knock on his door.

"Is everything okay?" Adele asks, harried, as she answers the door. I get the distinct impression she's been peeking from the lounge window ever since Taylor left her and the babies to come and help me, and I can't blame her.

"I need to ask you a question." I say, seeing myself into the sprawling home. The babies sit in bouncers in front of an enormous television screen that isn't switched on. Classical music plays on a low volume.

"They say it's good for brain development." Adele explains. "I can't stand the stuff but I've been trying to let them listen for 30 minutes a day. Just so you don't think I'm a pompous lawyer who listens to classical music. I honestly don't know my Beethoven from my... well... pick any other classical artist, person, thing!"

I laugh. Adele is such a welcoming character. I want to spend more time shooting the breeze with her, cuddling her babies over hot or tepid drinks, getting to know how her brain and her heart work. But right now, I just need her brain, and I'm prepared for a long visit. I've heard that lawyers never give straight answers, and a straight answer is what I need.

"Anyway, you need to ask me something? If it's about a woman's pelvic floor, yes the rumours are true, it goes to hell."

"Erm, it's not about a pelvic floor actually, whatever that

is." I say. "It's a legal question. I don't know what kind of law you did? Do? I hope you can help."

"I'll do my best but my baby brain seriously feels like I've forgotten like 98% of everything I know, and I've never claimed to know that much to start. I was more of a, know where to find the facts kind of lawyer, not a memorise the facts kind of lawyer, you know?"

"Uh-huh." I agree, but I don't know. My idea of being able to find the facts is typing a question into a search engine and hoping for the best. Surely lawyers can't follow that system too. Not while charging $500 an hour. Surely?

"So...?"

"Right. Yeah. So, this is just between us, if that's okay? It's a little bit personal and I –"

"I tell Taylor nothing, don't worry." Adele says with a wink.

"OK, thanks, good. So, let's say I have some money or something to pass on after I die. Could I give it with conditions on it, like they had to do certain things to get it? Or if something happened, they could lose it? Is that even possible?"

"Oh, yeah." Adele says, debunking my thoughts about lawyers not giving straight answers. "Totally. See it all the time. People love control."

"So, how would it work?"

"Well, whatever it was would be included in your Will, and your Will would just specify the conditions. It could be, like, won't inherit until a certain age, that's the most common one, but it could be anything really."

"Could it be that they lose the money if they got in trouble with the law?"

"Mm-hmm." Adele says, walking across to the music system and turning the power off. "Sorry, that music is driving me insane. I'll take crying babies over that. But yeah, totally. You got someone you need to motivate to stay on the straight and narrow, it can be really powerful."

"I imagine." I say. Adele is watching me, waiting for more detail. I silently apologise to Sandy and Coral, Sage's daughters. "My nieces."

"Agh, that's the worst." Adele says with a conspiratorial wink.

21

SAGE

*R*ydell Grove is a hippie's worst nightmare. I avoid the place, although the hot dog vendor on Smith Street has this dimple when he smiles that makes it almost tolerable when I do end up across this way.

It's one of those towns that is desperate to be a city, ya know? All high rise developments, people with briefcases who really have nowhere to rush to, and a mayor who is hungry for their little small town news to get some national coverage.

But tonight, I'm here with Patton Davey, who actually complimented me on my hair when he picked me up. Well, he asked if I'd had it cut. Which I clearly haven't. But I have curled it and that makes it look shorter, so he was close. I guess the Sheriff pays a little attention to more than just law breakers, huh.

The police station is empty, lights out, car park deserted. Which proves my point about the place being a small town. I'm pretty sure the cop shops across New York don't close so everyone can go home for grilled cheese suppers.

There's something about seeing a building like this in

the dark. Something that's plain wrong, and unsettling. I move a little closer to Patton, who side-glances at me and narrows his eyes. He's in work mode now. No more comments about my hair.

"Stay close." He commands, as if I was going to do anything but.

The station is small, I know that from when I ventured out this way for an organic food fayre a few years ago, stalls of expensive cheeses and enormous home grown zucchini all set up in the police station parking lot for some crazy reason. Every time a cop walked through the crowd with a hot dog (from the dimpled vendor) and a takeout coffee, they looked at the ground guiltily before disappearing back into the little station. But in the dark this place is cavernous. The cells, in particular, terrify me. Nobody stays there overnight, in fact I suspect they're barely used at all, but I have to force myself to look away from them before my imagination runs too wild.

I had my dabbles with the law when I was younger, experimenting with things I shouldn't, peer pressure causing me to try things, say things, do things I wouldn't have considered when with my more sensible sister. But I managed to avoid the police. I never set foot in a police station, never got a warning from a stern officer, and never had to go in a cell. But it was touch and go for a while. My need for an adventure, that longing to live a life bigger than my parents', it had me confused for a while about what kind of adventures I wanted to end up having.

"You listening?" Patton grunts.

I shake the thoughts from my head. "Sorry, I was distracted."

"God damn it, Sage." Patton curses. "I thought you were taking this seriously?"

"I am." I protest. "This place spooks me."

"We are the spooks, remember?" Patton says, and then he flashes me the most dazzling smile I might ever have seen. Or in the last fifteen years at least.

I grin. "Sorry, Sheriff, I'm listening. What were you saying?"

"I'll find the file and then we can split it, okay? You just need to read through as much as possible."

"What are we looking for, exactly?" I ask as we enter a room filled with filing cabinets. My lack of experience hangs heavy on my shoulders, like a winter coat.

Patton shrugs. "You can never tell. Just consider everything and let me know if anything doesn't add up."

I nod, unconvinced, as he hands me a small brown folder of papers. I set them out on a corner desk piled high with papers, half-full coffee cups and an ashtray full of cold cigarette butts.

"You get started there, I'm going to look for more." He commands, and moves away. He must see the panic in my eyes because he moves closer for a moment and reaches out, touches my arm. "I won't leave you."

I nod, one up-down motion, not trusting myself to do anything more. If you've heard people talk about chemistry, they were making it up, okay? Because nobody has ever felt the way I did when Sheriff Davey just touched my arm. The electrics in the room flicker, and the lamppost across the street extinguishes itself. That's when you know there's chemistry. And by Patton's swift retreat towards the file cabinets, he felt it too.

I gulp and force myself to open the brown folder, ignoring the desk clutter as best I can. Whoever calls this their workplace is a pig. It'll be a man, of course. A man who grew up with a mother fetching and carrying for them and expects life to always offer them the same service. I shake my head and glance at the first sheet of paper.

"There's an incident report." I call out across the room. Patton is scouring every file within the cabinets, file by file, drawer by drawer. "What are you doing?"

"Things get misfiled." He says with a shrug. "What does the report say?"

"Not much." I say. Most of the boxes on the double-sided sheet of paper are blank, incomplete. There isn't even a date. "It says it's a homicide, it's definitely about Lola, but nothing's really been filled out. How can that be?"

"It's not a Rydell problem." Patton says, slamming one drawer closed and opening the next. "They'll be busy on their own cases."

"What? Like, littering?" I ask. "Nothing ever happens here."

He sighs. "They probably don't know what to do with a murder, in fairness."

"And you do?" I ask, then cover my mouth as I realise how the question sounds. "I mean, have you ever -"

"No." He admits. "First murder case. But I want to catch the killer. These guys want to stick the papers in a drawer and forget it."

I can't argue with that.

Form-filling has never been my idea of a fun way to spend time, but even I can tell that the paperwork in this folder is woefully inadequate. A DUI probably gets more attention than Lola's murder has, and as insufferable as she was with her natural beauty and her disregard for people's feelings, she deserves more than that.

I move on from the incident report. The next few pages are sheets of yellow legal pads, each with a scribbled note on.

"Well, I think I've cracked it." I say, reading one of the sheets. "John from Thompson Road saw a UFO on the night in question. He didn't actually see any aliens but he imagines they were here, and they took Lola's body with them for human cloning purposes so they can invade Earth."

"Ah, good old John from Thompson Road." Patton says with a wry smile.

"You know this guy?"

"Every cop in a hundred kilometer radius knows him. He's been calling in after every crime for as long as I can remember, UFO this, alien that. The man's a nut job."

"Says the ghost Sheriff." I tease. "Plenty of people describe Connie the same way for believing ghosts exist."

Patton grins. This is why I love him. I mean, you know, love him in a platonic, working-together-on-a-murder-investigation kind of way. He doesn't take himself too serious.

"Anything else in there? Apart from John?" He asks.

I rifle through the papers, struggling to read some of the awful handwriting, then turn my attention back to the incident report. It staggers me that a trained police officer has left this file, in this state, to gather dust in a file cabinet. I sigh and continue inspecting each new sheet in turn.

"Ada Green?" I ask, reading from a second incident report within the file. "That name mean anything to you?"

"Nope." Patton says. "What is it?"

"An incident report, but it's from a robbery. Wait, it's seven years old. Does someone think there's a link between the two?"

Patton comes over to me, inspects the sheet over my shoulder. He's so close I can feel his breath on my neck. If I wasn't a married woman, well... that's my business.

"Hmm." He murmurs, taking the sheet from me. "Strange."

"It is, right?" I say, watching him.

"I don't know why anyone would have connected the two. Different crimes, different towns - this one happened here in Rydell, see - and Ada Green was a lot older than Lola, so it doesn't suggest a targeting of young women, for example."

"It doesn't make sense." I say.

"Hold on." He says, and turns the sheet over to examine the second side. In huge letters, a message has been scrawled across the back of the paper. "There's no connection. This poor woman's report was just used as scrap paper. Probably the closest thing this scruffy idiot had around when he took the call."

"So it's not even relevant." I say, dejected. The file's empty now, there's nothing else to go on.

"The report isn't, but the note here definitely is." Patton says, and he hands the paper back to me.

INC. CALL, TROY MONTAG, REF: LOLA ANTI. EYE WITNESS. CALL BACK REQ'D.

I gasp. "Troy Montag?"

Patton nods. "Has Connie spoken to him?"

"I don't think so." I say. "An eye witness, that means...."

"He saw what happened."

22

CONNIE

*S*age warned me not to do this, but for once I decided to be the carefree, rebellious sister and go against her advice. *Fine*, she'd said, and floated away in a temper. Probably off to find Patton Davey. They've been spending a lot of time together lately.

I wish she was here now, though, as the door bell rings and I pad across the hallway. I glance in the consultation room as I pass, do a quick sweep of the room with my eyes: the room's clear, two glasses of water are ready in place. All okay.

"Welcome!" I call out as I open the door, hoping my enthusiasm convinces myself as much as my customer.

Devin Summer stands on my veranda in boyfriend jeans that hang from her waist, a cropped-top revealing a pale, concave stomach and an oversize hoodie. The bags underneath her eyes look as though someone has colored them with a gray marker pen, and her skin is like a moon crater up close. I've always said that money makes people more attractive, or affords them the tools to trick the world into thinking they're more attractive, and proof of my theory is standing right before me. Although, of course, I know little about the supermodel world and this could be the look that's in this season.

She doesn't smile, and I force myself not to read anything into that. Lots of first-time clients don't smile. This is a nerve-wracking, hopeful, amazing, devastating experience.

"Come on in." I encourage, opening the door wide. "Don't stay out there, looks like a storm is on the way."

The clouds have been building all day, and they've formed a solid cover now, blocking out the blue sky and the sunshine. There's no rain, no wind even, but the birdsong sounds like more of a warning than a celebration, and the temperatures are impossibly humid. Any moment, the sky will be illuminated with a strike of lightning, I can tell.

I love the weather patterns here, the predictability of the seasons. We'll enjoy a wonderful summer, and a colourful fall, the snow will descend for winter and spring will promise new beginnings. In Waterfell Tweed, the only thing I could know with any certainty was that the wind would blow. Day after day after day.

"Come on through here." I say as I lead Devin through to the consultation room. I feel as though I'm coddling a small child, encouraging them to put one foot in front of the other. Is the supermodel really so used to having a staff that she can't even make basic conversation without guidance?

"I do insist that we only drink water during the consultation." I say as I sit down across from her. She shows no sign that she's heard me.

"I think you've brought something that belonged to your loved one?" I prompt.

She nods and reaches into the pocket of the hoodie that is unzipped and hangs over her body and across onto the couch on both sides of her. She looks tiny, waif-like, set aside the proportions of the furniture. The couch isn't even that big.

She holds out her fist to me, and I reach across, accept whatever she's offering. She drops a heavy gold band into the palm of my hand.

"This is beautiful." I say.

She doesn't react. Maybe she's a skeptic, one of those who believes it's all a con, that I'm picking up on every reaction she gives to allow me to guess why she's here. I get those sometimes. They're impossible to deal with. Not because I need their reactions, but because they give closed energy, which is hardly a great invitation to extend to their best friend or their second uncle or whoever it is they want to contact.

I run through the normal procedure and rules while I stroke the ring with my thumb and forefinger. I'm buying time, because Devin has brought negative energy into my home and whoever she is calling from the spirit world is ready to bring the same.

I take a deep breath. "This is your sister. Her name is..." I stumble over the word, seeing the general shape of it's letters but not the clear, focused form.

"Hadleigh." The spirit says, arriving with such energy that Devin herself gasps. She is the double of her sister, but while Devin carries a dark energy that is sadness and guilt, Hadleigh carries a fury.

"She's here, isn't she?" Devin asks, and I see the fear in her eyes.

I nod. "Hadleigh, Devin is here to speak to you. Devin, you can speak to Hadleigh directly, she can hear you. I'll feed her comments back to you."

Devin begins to shake and wraps the hoodie around her,

covering her flat stomach. "Can you tell her... oh, ok, I just talk. Hadleigh? I'm sorry."

Devin bursts into tears and I feel some of the dark energy around her release, seep out of the house through every open window, every air vent.

I watch Hadleigh, who stands by the door, simmering. Her anger is palpable.

I sit, and I wait.

Whatever is happening here, I'm simply the vessel who can channel Hadleigh's responses.

Devin cries for several minutes, covering her face with her hands, gently sobbing into her lap. I sip water and watch her and Hadleigh as closely as I can.

"I'm so sorry." Devin whispers.

"Ask her why." Hadleigh commands.

"Your sister asks why." I say. My stomach churns. There are days when I love my work, when I get to reunite people who love each other and allow them to share declarations of undying love. And then there are days when the conversations I am asked to facilitate are much harder, more complicated, more painful.

"Tell her... I... I'm sorry for the crash." Devin says, choking back a sob. She gazes at me, as if I am channeling her sister internally. Another common misconception. The TV world of charlatan mediums has a lot to answer for.

"Tell her I want her to explain what happened. I want to hear her tell the whole story and take responsibility. Accept it was her fault." Hadleigh is stone, no sympathy. A hard heart in a beautiful body.

I relay the message and Devin nods.

"I knew she'd want that." She says. She can't meet my gaze now. "It's why I've been too scared to come. I, erm... we, were both models."

"You can tell her to take my pictures down." Hadleigh interrupts, her voice pure venom. The pictures, I realise. Sage didn't see pictures of Devin all over her house, they were pictures of Hadleigh. A shrine to the sister who seems to hate her.

I choose not to pass on that message, pretending I haven't heard.

"It was a stupid party. I didn't even want to go, but there was this guy who was going to be there. Darren something, I don't even remember. He'd been trying to get together with us for a while, he wanted to shoot us for a perfume ad. So we went. And he didn't have a perfume ad, he was just a guy who knew the right people and said the right things. He was a complete waste of time. I was so freaking annoyed that I'd got ready and gone out for him." Devin says. She pauses, takes a sip of water, coughs to clear her throat. "I couldn't find Hadleigh, so I had a beer. And then she rocks up, bored by the party, desperate to leave right away. Everything had to be right away with Hadleigh. I should have told her no. I should have called a cab. I should have done a million things but I got in the car and I drove us home."

"Not quite home." Hadleigh spits.

"Not quite home." Devin says, and I wonder if their twin connection remains in place. Devin begins to cry again, tears escaping her eyes as she looks up and to the side as she remembers. "I swerved off road and hit a tree. Hadleigh was... she... they said it was instant, no pain. I hope that's right. The emergency services came and I think they were so shocked, I mean this was in the middle of our biggest runway show so we were pretty well recognised, I think they were stunned. Nobody breathalyzed me. It didn't really occur to anyone, I don't think."

I nod. It's not my place to judge.

"I would have passed, if they had. It was just one beer. But I don't remember swerving, and I've tried to. I've really tried to force myself to remember what happened and I can't." Devin says as a shudder passes through her body. She takes a sip of the water, gulps it too quick mid-tears and almost chokes. I'm ready to jump up and offer whatever rudimentary First Aid I've learnt from medical dramas on TV, but she recovers, cheeks red, eyes wild. "I think I fell asleep."

"Wow." I say, needing to give some reaction because Hadleigh remains silent.

"I miss her every day." Devin says. "She was my best friend my whole life. She was better at everything than me. More confident, more popular. More comfortable in her skin. The modelling was her idea. She was approached at a soccer game and came home and convinced me to go with her. I hated it at first, standing and posing. I'd struggled for so long with my acne, the last thing I wanted was to have pictures taken of me. But it started being fun, spending that time with her. I knew I was the awkward one compared to her, but I didn't care."

"Hadleigh, do you have anything to say?" I prompt. Hadleigh looks at me, and for a moment I see how her shoulders have slumped, how she looks at her sister. And then something hardens and her posture straightens, her eyes glass over.

"Sure." Hadleigh says, and something about the combination of her icy blonde hair and clear blue eyes is chilling. "Tell her she's a killer."

The words cause me to shiver, and Devin looks at me curiously.

"Your sister's struggling to come to terms with what happened." I say diplomatically.

Devin nods and begins to cry again. "I can't believe she's actually here. I never thought I'd get to be around her again. Then I heard about you, and I knew I had to come."

"You know, this might be enough for now." I say with a gentle smile. "This is a lot to take in, and such an emotional thing to discuss. Why don't you get some rest and maybe come back another day?"

Devin looks at me, her eyes wide. "Does she want me to go?"

"It's not that." I say, shifting in my seat. "But, honey, you look exhausted. I have a duty to look out for my clients, and the spirits too. This kind of conversation is hard for everyone."

Me included, I think. I'm ready to lie down in a darkened room with some relaxing nature sounds playing until I fall asleep and, hopefully, dream of anything but this sorry situation.

"I just needed to ask her." Devin says.

"I know." I say, with more urgency, because I need this meeting to end. The dark energy is growing. I need Hadleigh out of my house. "And today has been a really productive first appointment. You've made contact with your sister. That's huge, isn't it?"

Devin nods and drinks the last of her water, but makes no effort to get up off the couch.

"I just..." She begins, then takes a long, quivering sigh. "I just wanted to ask one thing."

"Okay." I say, settling back down into the comfort of the couch. She's going nowhere yet, that's clear. "Well, sure."

Devin looks right at me, then runs a slender hand through her hair.

She is building up to something, and Hadleigh remains by the door, like a coiled spring, ready to attack.

Don't ask, I silently implore. *No good can come of this.*

"Can she forgive me?" Devin asks, and I see how much the question has cost her. How much more comfortable the wondering must have been for her, compared to this moment, this raw moment of vulnerability, where the answer is about to be revealed.

I glance across at Hadleigh, who nurses her head as if the fatal wound continues to hurt. Which it may. Ghost pains, they're called.

Please, I silently pray. *Please give her this gift.*

Hadleigh moves across the room, standing directly in front of Devin.

"Please forgive me." Devin repeats.

Hadleigh smiles, her face returning to how it must have looked as a child. Sweet innocence, freckles, natural beauty.

"Please." Devin begs.

"Never." Hadleigh answers.

23

CONNIE

"*H*ow dare you?" She sneers, advancing towards me. Just days ago, I would have been upset by this encounter but not fearful. I thought I had no reason to fear spirits, but now I know. They can attack. They can hurt.

And I have one of the angriest spirits I've ever seen, in my house, refusing to leave.

"I had to." I say, trying to stand tall and appear confident.

"You had to lie? What's the point even calling out to me if you'll just lie your way through a meeting anyway? She needs to know the truth!"

"Does she?" I ask. "Why? What do you think that will do to her?"

"Well, it won't kill her, that's for sure." Hadleigh says. "So she'll still be ahead of me."

"Hadleigh, please. She's your sister."

"She's my killer." Hadleigh spits.

I see Patton and Sage appear in the kitchen, together of course. They really need to be a little more discreet, if you ask me. Atticus appears a few moments after and the three of them watch, assessing how out-of-hand the situation is.

"I'm asking you to leave." I repeat. I've already asked her four times since Hadleigh left, the smile of relief on her face.

Of course she forgives you, I'd said, every word costing me a professional self-respect. I don't lie. I don't take what the spirits say and shape it into more comfortable, easier to accept, half-truths. I warn clients, when they book an appointment, yes your spirit might not answer the call, but there's another option - they might answer the call and leave you wishing they hadn't.

I've shared devastating revelations in this room. Secrets and truths that leave me feeling dirty, as if I've just read someone's most private journal or walked in on a couple's marriage counselling. After those meetings, I jump in a hot bath, the water hot enough to scald my skin, and cleanse myself, before doing the whole thing again the next day.

But I couldn't share this truth with Devin.

A truth more heartbreaking than any I've heard before.

And so I swallowed my professional duties, my personal commitment to make my contribution to this industry honest and ethical, and I lied. And I don't regret it.

"You think you just get to call me in here and then get rid of me when you've heard enough? It doesn't work like that." Hadleigh says.

"The appointment's finished." I say. "I know you're angry, but can't you see how sorry she is? Can't you see how much she misses you?"

"Mm-hmm, and that helps me how? End result, I'm still dead."

I sigh. "I'm so sorry for what happened to you, I really, truly am. You're a beautiful young woman, right at the start of her life. It isn't fair. But I don't see what you'd gain by telling Devin you don't forgive her."

"She asked the question." Hadleigh says. "It's not like I

went across to her house and scrawled all over her walls that I'll never forgive her. She came here. She asked the question. And you owed me the truth. Who the hell do you think you are to steal my voice?"

I shake my head and sigh.

She's right. I've done a terrible thing.

"I'm sorry." I say. "I thought it was for the best. And, if I'm honest, I just didn't have the guts to tell her the truth."

Hadleigh laughs, a mean little noise, while Sage advances towards her from behind, and places a hand on her shoulder. Hadleigh spins around. "What's going on?"

"We heard the noise." Sage says, doing a double-take at Hadleigh's appearance. "Wow, you're Devin's twin."

"Her dead twin."

"Why so angry?" Sage asks. I roll my eyes. Just as I'm desperate for the conversation to end, she's going to get the whole thing started again. "I mean, we're all dead here... apart from Connie. Take a chill pill?"

Hadleigh stiffens for a moment, stunned by Sage's cheek, and then vanishes into thin air.

"Are you kidding me? I've been trying to get rid of her for a good twenty minutes."

Sage shrugs. "You were giving her the attention she wanted. Nothing like a bit of patronising to get rid of someone with an ego. Anyway, are you ready to sit down? We have news."

I don't even have to ask who the *we* refers to, and I walk out of the consultation room, closing the door behind me, and take a seat at the kitchen island.

"So, we went across to the station over in Rydell Grove." Patton says as Sage gazes up at him.

"I bet those buffoons didn't even have a file." Atticus says. He'd always had a strong rivalry with the neighboring towns, determined that they were weak impersonators of Mystic Springs.

"Well, almost. You should see the way they keep their desks over there. It's like a pigsty." Sage says. I try to resist the temptation to raise an eyebrow. Sage was never one for clean or tidy living, preferring to spend her time learning the lyrics to new songs and forever painting and repainting her toenails. In my memory of her alive, she's always barefoot. I guess she must have worn socks and shoes at some points, but my mind has blocked those out.

"It certainly is." Patton agrees. "But we worked hard and we did find a file."

"A file? You're kidding. Should we share this with Taylor?"

"One Sheriff's enough." Sage says, and Patton's chest swells.

"He still has Nettie in custody, guys." I remind them. "We have to work with him on this."

Sage rolls her eyes, but Patton nods.

"You're right." He says.

"I'll ring him."

**

When Taylor Morton arrives, he's in full Sheriff's uniform and the clothes, together with those dark-rimmed glasses, make him look awfully stern.

"There's been a development." I say when I open the door for him. He instinctively glances in every room as we walk through the hall way, then relaxes as we reach the kitchen at the back of the house. The holy trinity of investigative spirits, as I've come to think of them, stand by the counter, but he can't see them.

I switch on the kettle and open the cupboard that houses all of my drinks. I'm a specialty drink devotee, and I can right now offer Taylor any one of at least twelve flavored teas or, if he wants coffee, add a splash of almond, cinnamon or hazelnut syrup.

"Drink?" I offer.

To my eternal disappointment, he shakes his head. "I'm trying to quit caffeine."

I wrinkle my nose. "Why would you want to go and do that?"

He laughs. "I don't want to, trust me. I'm not getting any younger though... need to start looking after myself."

"Those twins must be keeping you up all night. Surely now's the time you need more caffeine."

"What is this, peer pressure to drink coffee?" He asks with a smile. "Damn it, I'll have a strong black. Don't tell my wife."

"It can be our secret." I say, grabbing my biggest mug and spooning four teaspoons of instant into it. That should give him a buzz to get through the day. "So... Nettie Frasier. You releasing her yet?"

"You know I can't tell you that." Taylor says, accepting the steaming cup of java.

"Well, we have some news for you." I say.

"We?" He asks.

"Patton's here, and Sage, and Atticus."

Taylor looks at me quizzically.

"Oops, you need introducing. Okay, so these are the spirits who started investigating things before you arrived in town. There's Patton, who you know, I believe?" I say. Taylor nods. "My sister, Sage, and Atticus is the former mayor of Mystic Springs."

"Is he the dude who invented the mystical healing properties of the springs?" Taylor asks as he takes a hungry sip of the black liquid. "Mm, this stuff's amazing. Adele will kill me."

"You sound like a junkie getting a hit." I tease.

"I feel like one!" He says. "The problem is, she's got too much space in her head now she's not working, and she's turning far too much of it onto how to improve me. No caffeine, daily runs, she's a demon."

"Anyway... Nettie?"

"Oh come on, Connie. You're killing me. Her house is still empty, isn't it? You can draw whatever you want from that. I can't discuss it."

"Okay." I say, making myself a hazelnut cappuccino. I'm aware the damn drink probably has more calories in than Taylor's allowed to eat in a day, and I plan on enjoying every single one.

"You said you have news?"

"Well, they do." I say, gesturing towards Sage and Patton. "Patton?"

Patton clears his throat. "There was a witness to Lola's murder, I can't see that he was ever spoken to."

"Wow. They're saying that there was a witness to Lola's murder."

"Who?" Taylor asks.

Patton tells me and I feel my insides churn.

"It's Troy. Troy Montag."

Taylor looks at me blankly.

"He's just a kid. He's the principal's son." I explain. I don't understand why but my stomach sinks at the thought of that sweet boy being involved in this horrid business.

"Can I... would you let me speak to him first? Please, Sheriff? He's just a kid."

Taylor purses his lips. "Connie, I have to take order in this town. That means interviewing my witnesses and running my cases without people interfering."

I blink at him.

He takes a breath and squeezes the bridge of his nose. "I don't like being the bad guy, trust me. I like you, and I think it's really sweet how you're making friends with Adele. But when I wear this uniform, I'm in charge. Geeze, that makes me sound like a horse sucking burger camper."

"Huh?" I ask.

He laughs. "I've got to give up cussing too. Makes for some pretty, erm, creative moments. Anyway, I just need you to let me do my job now."

I nod slowly. "Is the station all set for you, Sheriff?"

The local police station has been on lock down ever since Patton Davey died and left the position vacant. I'll drive by occasionally and see teenagers sitting in the parking lot eating burgers out of brown paper bags, listening to country music on their phones with the volume as high as it'll go. That's about as wild as life in Mystic Springs gets for a teen on a Friday night.

"Should all be sorted in a few days." He says. "There's been some issue with the keys."

"I bet he's lost them. Moron." Patton mutters. I glare at him.

"So, maybe I could help in the meantime? I mean, a young kid like Troy, he'll open up more to someone he knows than a brand new Sheriff he's never met before." I say.

Taylor looks at me over his coffee mug as he takes another sip. "You're good. You should try working on hostage negotiation or something. But the answer's still no. And, I'll be honest Connie, I don't really appreciate being put in this position. I'll let it slide this time, but don't ask me again, okay? Thanks for the drink."

He sets his mug on the granite counter and gives me a nod, then stomps his way back through the house, seeing himself out.

"That man is so arrogant." Patton seethes.

Sage is predictably quick to agree with him. "He likes throwing his weight around, huh!"

"He's doing what any new Sheriff would do, guys, come on." Atticus says, the voice of reason as usual. "I seem to remember you having a similar conversation with Violet when you were new in town, Sheriff Davey."

"It's fine." I say, although my appetite for my cappuccino has gone. "It's not personal, I know he has to get the town to respect him."

"Yeah, and having an ego the size of Louisiana won't help." Patton mutters.

"Guys, I don't think making him the enemy is the best way forward." I say. "We need to work with him. Poor Nettie's in jail right now, and God knows where if our own station isn't open. He must have sent her across to Jefferson."

"So are you suggesting we sit back and wait until the keys to the damn station are found, and then wait for him to get around to speaking to Troy?"

"Of course not." I say. I might look jolly, in that way that overweight people are required to by society - don't get me started on that. But I'm a tough old broad, and I don't go down without a fight. "I said I'd help with this investigation, and that's what I'm going to do."

"Ooh, fighting talk." Sage squeals. "See, Sheriff, I told you my sister had a bit of fire in her belly."

"I never doubted it." Patton says, and it's right. Despite his belief that I was a charlatan, we actually got on well when he was alive. He even gave me the odd speeding ticket here and there, and it seemed to me like he respected the kind of woman who knew when to keep her foot on the gas.

"So, what are you going to do?" Atticus asks, gazing at me over his glasses.

I glance at the faces watching me expectantly, needing me to move this forward for them. Atticus, still hoping that the trail leads back to Desiree Montag for some reason. Patton, needing to solve the case before Taylor. And Sage, my darling Sage, along for the ride. As she has been all her life.

"I'm going to see Troy." I say, with a decisive nod.

24

SAGE

*D*esiree opens the door, still dressed in an oversized tee and flannel pyjama bottoms, her feet bare and revealing hot pink toenails.

"Connie?" She asks, stifling a yawn. It's nearly 10am, and the discovery that Desiree enjoys a lie-in feels scandalous.

"Sorry to disturb you." My sister says, cheeks flushed. "Is Troy in? It can't wait, I'm afraid."

Desiree holds the door open without another word, her body jumping to attention, recognising the alarm in our words. "What's wrong?"

"I just need to talk to him." Connie says as she enters. I float in behind her, feeling the chill of the idle radiators as I pass.

"Let me get him." Desiree says, heading for the staircase. She turns back to Connie. "Sorry, I've never been a shout-up-the-stairs kind of mom. Give me a minute."

"Sure." Connie says.

"See yourself into the snug." Desiree says with a cursory point towards the first room off the hall. We follow her command and find ourselves in a room outfitted in dark mahogany furniture, every wall aligned with books. A small TV sits in the corner of the room, the screen covered with a child's poster declaring - *BORED? DO SOMETHING!* - with bright felt tip drawings of the 'something' that could be done instead of watching TV; there's a child colouring, another riding a bike, another going for a walk, one at the park, and another carrying grocery bags for an old woman with white hair that barely shows up on the paper.

"Ugh, what a drag." I say as I take a close up look at the art work. It's signed as *Troy, age 5*. I wonder if he regrets that picture now, how he's created his own lack of TV watching.

"I think it's a good idea." Connie says. "We're too dependent on the TV nowadays. People don't read any more."

I screw my nose up. "Of course they do. You can do both, you know."

"But people don't." Connie says. "That's the problem. If I ask someone now whether they like Agatha Christie, they'll think I mean one of the dreadful Poirot adaptations that are nothing like the original stories."

I roll my eyes.

She sighs. "I just think it does no harm to turn off the TV a bit."

"Okay." I say, and I think back to the days when my daughters were young, the way that children's TV programming was only on for around an hour a day and how they made their own fun without it occurring to them to spend all day in front of the screen. There's so much choice now, a hundred channels, a hundred more on TiVo, there's no need to leave the room never mind the house. "Ya know, you're probably right."

Connie laughs. "You must have it bad, even agreeing with me about something."

"Have what bad?" I ask, turning to my sister. She raises

an eyebrow and purses her lips. "What? I don't know what you're talking about."

"Yes Sheriff, no Sheriff." She says as she bats her eyelashes.

I shake my head. "Don't be silly."

"Sage, I know what you're like when you have a crush."

"Oh, yeah, a crush." I say with a light flick of my pony-tail. "He's a fine looking man."

We silence at the sound of footsteps lightly coming downstairs. Desiree appears in the doorway a moment later, changed into beige slacks and a t shirt. She looks no more presentable than she did in her nightwear, really.

"He's just getting ready." She says. "Can I get you a drink?"

"I'm fine." Connie says with a smile. She's still standing up and she sinks down into the dark leather seat now, an action that Desiree mirrors. "But thanks."

"He doesn't seem to know why you'd be here." Desiree says.

"Oh, no. He wouldn't." Connie says. She smiles, ignoring the subtle request for more invitation, forcing herself to stay quiet. She isn't great with authority, always feels guilty around people with power even though she's never had anything to hide in her life, and she has to avoid eye contact to hold her tongue.

Desiree sits on her hands, her foot taps lightly on the wooden floor, until echoing footsteps boom on the staircase, and the door bursts open. Troy is wild-eyed, face still wet from a splash of water, dressed in a tracksuit, a slug of a moustache atop his lip.

"Yo, Connie." He says with a lazy smile. His eyes scan the room, pass me, check for anyone else present disturbing his weekend rest.

"Hey Troy." My sister says. She's got a soft spot for this kid, that's obvious to see. She loves kids, full stop, which makes it all the more irritating that she was never around for mine, but this man-child in his leggy body, he's special to her. I can't figure it out.

"What's this about?" Desiree asks, no time for pleasantries. A woman whose career depends on her advocacy skills. Always advocating, that's what she says if you ever hang around in the staff room at the high school. *I feel like I'm advocating more than I'm teaching.*

Not that I would know about that, of course. Although the school isn't a private dwelling, so I've got more permission to be there than I have to be here right now.

"Ok, so I'm here to warn you really." Connie says, addressing Troy, not Desiree. He nods in a way that suggests he has no idea what she means. "There's a new sheriff in town."

"Finally." Desiree says with a nervous smile. "But Troy isn't in any trouble. You're not in trouble, are you?"

"Of course not, mamma." He says, and he reaches across and holds her hand. I mean, the boy is a heart breaker.

"He's going to investigate Lola's murder, Troy. He's already started, and it turns out that Rydell Grove have a file on it. Do you know what their file says?"

Troy shakes his head but his face pales.

"It's got a call from an eye witness. You know what that is? Because my understanding, and maybe this is a British thing, it could be something else here. But my understanding is that that's someone who saw what happened."

"That's what it means here." Desiree says, her voice barely a whisper.

"There's a call from you, and it says you're an eye witness." Connie says.

Troy raises his head, pauses, then lowers it again. It's so slow, so thoughtful, you can't call it a nod. "I did call them. They never rang me back."

"I didn't think they had." Connie says with a sad smile. "But now we have a Sheriff again, he's going to come and speak to you. And I didn't want him to just turn up and worry you guys, I wanted to tell you first."

"I appreciate that." Desiree says and she lets out a long breath, stands and begins to pace the room.

"It's ok, mamma." Troy says. "I didn't kill Lola."

Desiree lets out a laugh. "Oh my goodness, my sweet boy, I know you didn't. But why didn't you tell me you'd seen something? You've been so quiet. I knew something was wrong."

He shrugs. "When they didn't call me back, I thought they'd decided I didn't know anything. It didn't seem worth talking about."

"They're just busy." Connie says.

"It didn't happen in their town." Desiree says. "I see it all the time. Not their territory."

"So what happens now?" Troy asks, his dark eyes focused on my sister.

"You don't need to do anything. In fact, I've been a bit naughty coming across here. I told the Sheriff I wouldn't, but I had to warn you." Connie says.

"We won't lie for you." Desiree says, sternly. "I won't let Troy lie for you. I appreciate the warning, Connie, but my boy can't cover for you."

"I wouldn't ask you to." Connie says. "I'm just letting you know when he comes, he'll think you haven't been spoken to already. Okay?"

Desiree nods then returns her focus to her son.

"So what did you see?" Desiree asks. "You need to tell me everything."

Troy takes a deep breath. "I didn't see anything."

"What?" She asks. "But you rang the police and told them you did? You know how serious it is to waste police time, boy."

"I wasn't wasting police time. That's my whole point, I was right there by the kitchen door the whole time, I was watching her, hoping she'd notice me but she never did. And then there was a bit of a scene, the spirits were floating through people, remember? So I glanced away, and when I looked back, she was dead."

"So someone went in while you were distracted?" Desiree asks. "I don't understand what you're saying."

"There wasn't time for anyone to go in, and all I did was look into the lounge instead of the kitchen. I was still right by the doorway. Nobody passed me."

"I don't get it."

But I do, and a chill runs through my body. I watch Troy, consider the way he checked the whole of the room when he entered, how his gaze is fixed on Connie and his mum. And I know.

Troy sighs. "You won't believe me."

"I will." Connie says, and she locks eyes on me as she speaks. I nod.

Troy coughs, stands and leaves the room. His footsteps are audible stomping up the stairs.

Desiree goes to follow him, but Connie reaches for her hand.

"Give him a minute." She urges.

Desiree throws her head back and runs her fingers through her dreads. "He's such a good kid. I don't want him messed up in this."

"He's a witness." Connie says. "Not a suspect. All he did is see something. Or not see something."

The stomping returns and Troy appears in the room, carrying a large pad of flip board paper. He hands it to his mum, open on a page heavy with charcoal.

"I thought you'd stopped drawing." She says, and her voice is the sting of every mother who feels their child slipping away from them.

He shrugs. "Not the point, mamma. Look."

And she does.

Connie stands and gathers in, and I follow, hanging back slightly so I don't crowd them.

The drawing is beautiful, but dark. It's the kitchen of the Baker house, and the detail is staggering. The window fittings look so authentic I'm almost tempted to close the shutters to keep the heat in. Sprawled on the floor is Lola Anti, and it's clear that her face is etched in Troy's mind, memorised over months of nursing a crush on her.

"What's this?" Desiree asks, pointing with a talon to a cloud of smoke in the corner of the kitchen. "Is this, like, her soul leaving her body or something like that?"

"No." Troy says.

That's not something you can see, I almost say, but now isn't the time to distract Connie. It does happen. But it isn't visible. Even to Connie. Even to spirits.

"What is it, Troy?" Connie pushes.

"That's the murderer." Troy says, his Adam's apple bobbing as he swallows. "That's who killed her."

"I don't get it." Desiree says.

"It's a spirit." Troy says, patient. "I saw them vanish. I didn't see who it was."

"But you..."

"You see spirits?" Connie asks.

Troy nods. "It started last year. I ain't told nobody."

"You..." Desiree stutters. She believes in hard facts. She does not believe in spirits. "But, honey, you know that's not all real. No disrespect, Connie."

Connie rolls her eyes.

"Mamma, I saw what I saw. I can see spirits. I mean, I know that Sage is here, for example." Troy says, and I grin at the mention of my name. He looks right at me then, gives a coy smile.

"Well, hello." I say.

"Why wouldn't you tell me?" Desiree asks. "Why wouldn't you share this?"

Troy fixes a stern look towards her. "Well, mamma. I guess we both have our secrets."

25

CONNIE

"*I* knew I had a connection with you." I say, attempting to move past the awkwardness between Troy and Desiree.

"I've wanted to talk to you about it." Troy admits. "I guessed you'd understand more than anyone else. It's so confusing."

"Has she been to see you?" I ask.

"Nah." Troy says with a shake of his head. "She never spoke to me. Didn't even know who I was."

"She was a pretty messed-up girl, ya know. You're probably better off that way." Sage says, and the dynamic of someone other than me being able to see and hear my sister is incredible. I'm not sure if I like it. All these years I've had her to myself.

"Yeah, I guess." He says.

Desiree has left us to talk, refusing to argue with her son after his mysterious comment about secrets. She drove off, saying she had school work to catch up on. Troy had said nothing more about it, and we hadn't asked.

"So, it started last year? How often are you seeing them?" I ask.

"Not all the time." Troy says. "I've tried to ignore it, kinda hoped it'd go away."

"I saw you check the room when you came in here." Sage says.

"Yeah, I do that all the time. I mean, I'm not really scared, but I like to know if someone's around, you know?"

I nod. "I did the exact same thing for a long time. I saw my first spirit when I was about your age."

"It's mad, isn't it?" Troy says. "I've never spoken to one before, not until today."

"Wow, I'm your first. I feel super special." Sage says with a grin.

"Well, that's good." Troy says, with an apologetic smile. "Connie, when the Sheriff comes, he's not going to believe me, is he?"

"Oh." I say, remembering the blood across Taylor's face after Lola hit him. "I think he will actually. He's pretty open-minded."

"I wish I'd seen more. I mean, I can't tell you who the murderer is."

"Look, you've done everything you can." I say. "You were really brave contacting the police, especially since nobody knew about your gift."

"It doesn't feel like a gift." Troy says.

"I know." I repeat. "I know it doesn't at first. And even when you're used to it, sometimes it's a real pain. But you can use it for good. And I'm here to help you get your head around it all."

"Thanks, Connie." Troy says.

I stand up and pull him in for a hug, then release him. "You're gonna be okay if we head off?"

"Sure." He says. "Thanks for the warning. About the Sheriff coming."

**

As we stroll back across town, I see movement at Nettie's home. A Buick sits idling on the drive while a short man in a suit, holding a briefcase in his hand, stands on the veranda.

"Can I help?" I call across to him. He turns, mistakes me for the homeowner, and speeds across the lawn towards me, hand outstretched.

"Mrs Frasier, my absolute pleasure to see you."

"I -" I begin, but this man has no time to spare.

"Can't stop, awfully busy, please take this."

"Excuse me?" I say as he thrusts an envelope in my hand.

"Consider yourself served. We'll see you in Court. And, please, have a marvellous day!" He says, then dashes across the lawn and back into his car, where the engine is still running. He has reversed out of the drive before I've even had chance to register what's happened.

"Why didn't you tell him you're not Nettie?" Sage asks.

"Are you serious?" I ask. Sometimes I wonder what planet my sister is from. "You saw what just happened, there was no time."

She shrugs. "You should have just told him."

"Ugh!" I groan, then glance at the envelope in my hand. Addressed to Mrs D Frasier, as if marriage got rid of her own first name, there's a return address stamp on the back for a firm of city lawyers.

"Well, you should open it." Sage says.

"I'm pretty sure it's an offence to open someone else's mail."

"Not when that person is incarcerated." Sage says, and she may have a point. Even a law dunce like me knows that if something is served on you personally, it's pretty important. And who else is going to open it for her?

"Fine." I say, tearing into the envelope, then glancing around me. "Not out here, though. Let's go home."

**

Back home, Sage floats next to me as I pull the papers from the thick envelope.

Legal documents.

I stare at them for minutes but I can't make sense of what it means.

"I have to get an appointment to visit Nettie." I say.

Sage nods. "I can't see Sheriff Bighead agreeing to that."

"Sage, he really isn't that bad. He's just doing his job."

"Whatever." She says.

I shake my head. There are days when I think one lifetime is enough to have spent with my sister, and today's one of those days.

"What is it anyway?"

"I don't know." I admit.

"Let me see." Sage says, and I hand the papers to her. She inspects the front page, then the rest. "Wow. Lawyers earn so much but can't use simple English. It's like they design it so you can't understand it."

"I know." I agree. "Maybe I could ask Adele to help us?"

Sage pulls a face. "I don't think so. Remember who she's married to."

"True." I say. I don't doubt Adele's ability to keep things private, but I don't want to put her in an awkward position.

"I know." I say. It's a longshot, but worth a try. I pick up my cell phone and dial the number. The receptionist answers immediately, despite it being a Sunday - this must be a very expensive city firm, I think. I can picture her, with her sing song voice, sitting in a 25th floor office surrounded by glass, feeling literally on top of the world.

"Oh, hello. It's Nettie Frasier here, I've been served with papers this morning but I'm struggling to understand them. Can I speak to someone?"

"Please hold." The receptionist says. Instead of hold music, I'm connected to an automated message that describes the accolades of the law firm and their staff. Cases won. Articles published. Laws changed. Minutes pass. "Mrs Frasier, forgive the delay? I've just logged in to the case system? I think you're referring to the asset forfeiture application?"

It's hard to tell if she's really asking a question, as all of her sentences end with what sounds like a question mark.

"It's the documents served today."

"Please hold." She says, throwing me back into the message of their staggering accomplishments. I don't need a lawyer and even I'm tempted to hire them. "The case system is showing service of an asset forfeiture application only? I hope that helps."

"Well, no." I say, conscious of how dull my own voice seems compared to this woman. "I don't know what the papers mean."

"Please hold." She says, and I groan. "It's definitely an asset forfeiture application?"

"I just need to know what that means."

"Oh." The woman says. "You don't know what it means?"

"No." I say, feeling about as stupid as I ever have in my life.

"It's an application to have your assets forfeited." She says, as if that settles it. The sing sing has gone from her voice. "You'll already be aware of this, Mrs Frasier. It's clearly explained in the Will."

"And what happens then? Where do they go?" I ask.

"Into Trust, of course, for Mr Frasier?" She sings.

"Mr Frasier is dead." I say.

She laughs. Actually laughs. "For now."

**

Taylor agrees to a meeting when I explain the situation. Urgent mail, personally delivered.

Nettie is housed in the Jefferson County jail, as I'd guessed. They have a problem with drunks and their cells are always in demand, meaning they're the only town out of the three of us who keep a police presence available 24/7. Sure, after 6pm it consists of one divorced guy who orders in pizza and shares it with the inmates, but it's more than Mystic Springs or Rydell Grove have after hours.

Nettie looks fabulous, of course. In a staggering display of small-town policing, she's been allowed to keep her belongings in the cell with her, and it turns out her handbag holds a full spare set of make-up. She sits, poised, in a cell and barely reacts when I appear, as if there's as much chance I'm arriving because of my own arrest as there is me being there to visit her.

I've never spent as much time with her as I have since Lola was killed, so her lack of warm welcome isn't surprising.

"Hey." I say. I've been allowed to speak to her from the other side of the bars, and with the desk officer listening in on every word from his desk, where the cold remnants of last night's pizza remain. "How are you holding up?"

"Oh, ya know." She says with a shrug, which isn't really an answer at all.

"You've got some mail." I say, handing the envelope through the bars to her. "I opened it, sorry. I didn't know if they'd let me visit, and I thought it was important."

"Let me guess." She says, without looking at the contents. "Asset forfeiture."

I nod frantically. "Yes! You're expecting it?"

"No, not exactly. They're being a little ahead of themselves. I've not been convicted."

I wait, curious for details.

She sighs. "If I'm convicted of an offence, everything I inherited from Desmond's Will goes back into Trust."

"Wow." I say. "I've never heard of that before."

"Nobody has. But it's allowed. It's watertight. He's like the gift that just keeps on giving."

"But who else would he want to have his money?"

"Nobody." Nettie says. "He wants it protected for himself."

"What?"

Nettie laughs. "He's been frozen. He's convinced he'll be coming back to life, when the technology's there. This way, his money will be waiting for him."

I shake my head, because I've heard some things in my time, but this is mad.

"His body's been frozen?"

She nods. "It's not that unusual. Lots of people who have the money are doing it."

"Wow."

"I know." Nettie says. "I just hope I'm dead before he comes back. I had more than enough of him when he was alive."

"We need to make sure you're not convicted." I say, feeling a desperate need to fight for this woman who has already been wronged by the man who should have loved and supported her. She deserves a break.

"Connie." She says, staring at me. "They found the murder weapon in my garbage. You saw me with it. I have motive. I think we all know the way this is going to go. And." She takes a deep breath. "They're going to reopen Desmond's death. They'll try to get me for both."

I gulp, because I know this is true. I've heard Taylor discuss it, and Patton has told me it's the obvious way forward. Desmond's own death, never considered to be suspicious at the time it happened, suddenly looks awfully convenient when you factor in Lola's murder as well.

Suddenly, Nettie Frasier with her flawless skin and her perfect dress sense, looks like a wife who was trying a little too hard for wedded bliss. When her husband's head was turned by a young temptress, it was more than she could stand. And they both had to be punished.

It's such an enticing story.

I can see the newspaper headlines now.

26

CONNIE

*T*he Town Hall is bustling with the crack of anticipation and excitement. Nothing like this has happened before. Nothing like this has been attempted before.

I look out of the front door towards the full moon and then close the door. Close us in.

I lock the doors and turn to the packed congregation. Troy meets my eyes, terror upon his face, and I give him as reassuring a smile as I can manage, as I survey the crowds. It's standing room only.

I stand nervously on stage, understanding how uncomfortable Desiree must feel when she has to address a crowd.

She sits beside Troy now, holding his hand. The school staff take up the rest of her row. Mariam is by her other side.

"Ready?" I ask Violet, who sits on a chair on the stage. She grins at me through a pair of neon orange glasses. I have no idea if the woman needs any help to see or if glasses are just a way of adding yet another colour to her outfit.

She stands, and slowly the crowd register her movement and begin to hush themselves.

She raises her arms, hands outstretched, palms upwards.

"This won't surprise some of ya." She says with a cackle, for she is about to reveal a secret she has sheltered her whole life. A secret I had no right to ask her to share. As she moves her arms higher and higher, the audience are rapt, the room is perfectly silent. She begins to chant gently under her breath. The room darkens.

Sage appears first, confused.

"Mystic Springs for you tonight, one and all I give you sight." Violet chants, again and again and again, her voice increasing. A nervous energy travels through the crowd.

"She's a witch!" Someone says in a whisper that carries across the room.

Patton arrives a moment later, by Sage's side.

Someone in the audience gasps and points. The people nearby turn to look, some scream but they are hushed by others in the crowd who simply stare, stunned, at the spirits.

More spirits arrive, until the room is packed.

Atticus goes to Mariam, who sobs instantly, able to see him for the first time since he passed. She cries so much her whole body shakes. I look away. Tonight, I must think, not feel.

"Ladies and gentlemen." I call out, spotting Adele and Taylor in the front row with a baby in each of their arms. "We're here tonight because one of us is a murderer."

The crowd gasp. One person tries to get out of the door at the back of the hall, realises its locked, returns to their seat.

"The only way we can solve this crime is if we are all joined, for one night only. Yes, you can see spirits. Yes, they are real. This is no trick. The spirits mean you no harm. Please, don't be alarmed."

"You said one of us is a murderer!" A voice calls out from the crowd.

"Yes, I did." I say. "But not one of you."

I press a button on the small remote I have in my hand, and a photograph of Lola Anti appears on the projector screen.

"Nettie Frasier is currently in custody for the murder of Lola Anti." I announce. The crowd begin to gossip between themselves. "She didn't commit that murder. But I know who did."

Sage rushes forward and people move out of her way, shield themselves from her. "What are you doing? This is dangerous."

But everyone can hear her, and she's spent too long not being heard. The attention is more than she can handle, and she retreats from the stage, back into the crowd, to hide.

"I've been helped by Patton Davey, our former Sheriff, and Atticus Hornblower, our former Mayor. They're here now. I was asked to help them investigate, because they needed a living person to interview living people."

The crowd all spin in their seats, attempt to pick out Patton and Atticus in the crowd. I gesture towards them both to come up to the stage, and they do, to a round of applause.

"We miss you!" Someone calls out to them both.

"I'm trippin', man." A college student drawls to the friend who sits beside him as he rubs his eyes to check if this is real.

"What we didn't know then." I continue. "Is that the murderer isn't amongst the living."

The community take in my words and a silence falls, among the living and the spirits.

"Lola was killed by a spirit. A spirit who couldn't stand seeing..."

"You said they mean us no harm."

"These spirits don't." I say. "The spirit in question isn't here. That spirit has a power that is too strong for Violet alone. I've given you sight, now, so that we can all come together. I need everyone in the room to work together and chant with Violet, to call in the spirits who don't want to be here."

"Why would we call in a spirit who's dangerous?" Someone calls out.

"Because we can't stop what we can't see." I say.

"Join in, it's nice and easy." Violet says, returning to her feet. "We command all spirits far and near, command you now to appear."

"We command all spirits far and near, command you now to appear." I join in, trying to ignore the nerves in my stomach. This is our only hope. I just hope it works.

"We command all spirits far and near, command you now to appear." We continue, and the crowd begin to join in. I can pick out voices I know, some more confident than others. Mariam, speaking through sobs.

A woman squeals in the crowd and I look across to see more and more spirits arriving. The shy ones. The ones who wanted a peaceful afterlife. The ones who don't respond when I try to channel them for loved ones.

"We command all spirits far and near, command you now to appear." We continue, more and more voices joining in.

I look across the stage and see that the spirit I was waiting for has arrived.

Hadleigh searches the crowd for Devin, who attended reluctantly and seems to be one of the audience finding the gathering the most upsetting. She mutters the words, mouth barely moving, head fixed on the ground.

I nod towards Violet, who stops chanting and takes her seat. The crowd gradually realise she has stopped, and do the same. The way she commands an audience simply by choosing to start or stop speaking is amazing.

"Thank you." I say.

"What's the plan?" Patton whispers to me.

"Be on alert." I whisper back and he nods.

I look straight at the murderer, into eyes that are cold and an amused smirk. The familiar dark energy makes me shiver.

"What took you so long?" They ask, and the audience gasp.

"You killed Lola." I say, my voice trembling but somehow remaining loud and clear. Everyone needs to hear this. Their life is going to change forever because of this.

"And what are you going to do about it?" They ask, floating closer to me. I back up instinctively, moving towards to edge of the stage.

"We need the truth." I call, glancing behind me. I'm just a few steps away from a six foot drop.

"I'll tell you whatever you want to know." The person says with a laugh as they survey the crowd. "I have nothing to lose, do I? I've already lost it all."

"Help us understand." I say.

"There's nothing to understand."

The audience begin to mutter between themselves, speculation flying.

I sense someone approaching and turn to the side, see Desiree climbing the steps at the side of the stage. She comes over and stands by my side, gives me a reassuring nod.

"You shouldn't be up here alone." She whispers.

"Brave, Ms Montag." The spirit sneers. "We're up here sharing our secrets. Are you sure you want to join in?"

I think back to Troy's words. *I guess we both have our secrets.*

I feel Desiree begin to shake beside me and reach for her hand.

"Careful, Connie. Don't make Mariam jealous." The spirit says with a sneer. I squeeze Desiree's hand tighter but she pulls away from me and takes a step towards the spirit, back straight, chin up.

"I'm not scared. Not any more." She says, then looks out into the audience, her eyes finding Mariam. "I'm sorry, baby. I'm sorry for keeping you a secret when I'm so damn proud of you."

"I love you." Mariam calls to Desiree.

"I love you more." Desiree says, and she blows a kiss to Mariam before returning her attention to the spirit on the stage. "Your turn, Desmond."

He laughs. "Nettie was spending my money. I had to stop it."

"It was her money. It was all left to her." I call across to him.

"She didn't earn a cent of it. It's mine!" He shouts, cheeks flashing red.

"So you framed her?" I ask.

"I had to." He says. "When I saw her argue with Lola, it was too good an opportunity. I'm an investment banker. I look for opportunity and then get in quick. It's what I do. So I did it."

"How could you kill Lola? What had she ever done to you other than love you?" I ask.

This makes him laugh hysterically. "Love? That girl knew nothing about love. It was a business deal."

"But still, she'd done nothing wrong to you."

"I guess not." Desmond says with a shrug, as if the question is only just occurring to him.

"I was good to you." A voice comes, and everyone turns. Lola Anti floats down the walkway, people ducking out of her way as she passes. She joins us on stage and glares at Desmond. "I was better than you deserved."

"Well." He says with a smile. "That's a common theme from my life."

"You're a monster." Lola says, and her words hang in the air.

"You knew what you were getting into, little girl." Desmond taunts. "You had a good ride. All your bills paid. Pocket money to spend. It wasn't going to last forever."

"Desmond Frasier, you murdered Lola Anti." I call, voice steady now. I will get justice.

Desmond grins at me, his fox-like features relaxed. Untouchable.

"Yes, I did. And it's the perfect crime. Nobody's going to believe that a ghost killed someone. Nettie will rot in prison and when it's time, I'll be brought back to life and my money will be waiting for me. You fools will all be long gone by then, I expect."

"Atticus?" I call.

Atticus is by my side within a moment, nodding slowly.

"Desmond. We can't allow this behaviour in our spirit community." Atticus begins.

"Sit down, old man." Desmond says, advancing towards us. I step back again, too close to the edge of the stage.

Mariam is up from her chair in the audience, but Troy

grabs her and forces her to remain in place. I flash a grateful smile at him.

"You can't do anything now. You're not in charge any more." Desmond continues.

Atticus looks towards Patton, who nods.

"Desmond Frasier, a bench of your peers have considered your actions and feel we have no choice but to banish you."

"To what?" Desmond asks, incredulous.

"You will spend eternity in Nowhere."

Desmond laughs. "You must be kidding me."

"This is no joke." I say. "You've messed with the wrong town, Desmond."

Atticus holds out his arm, points at Desmond, who remains rooted in place, unable to move. "I pronounce you banished."

And with that, there is a pop of white light, a cloud of smoke, and he is gone. Forever.

The crowd begin to murmur between themselves, and then someone begins a round of applause.

I face the crowd, just a centimeter from having fallen off the stage, and await their silence.

"Ladies and gentlemen, for your own safety, we have no choice but to cast a spell over the whole of Mystic Springs. All living people will be able to see the spirits in this town now, for good."

There's a commotion as people turn to the person sitting next to them to check they've heard correctly.

"I quite like it." Mariam says, the first to talk above the general chatter.

Atticus returns to her side. She faces him, glances at Desiree, gives a nervous smile.

"I love you, my darling girl." He says, then turns his own

attention to Desiree. "And you? I thought you were taking advantage of her when I saw you out of work together. Unpaid overtime, you know. This is better." He says, stroking his beard. He nods. "Yes, this is much better. I don't want her to be alone."

"She won't be." Desiree says, beaming at Mariam.

"That settles it then." Atticus says.

"Meeting dismissed." I call with a laugh. People begin to shift in their seats but nobody is in a hurry to leave.

"So, are you a witch then?" Someone calls out to Violet Warren.

She grins, pushing her bright glasses back up her nose. "That'd be telling."

*I*t takes precisely thirty-seven minutes before the first living person approaches me and tells me how beautiful I am.

I mean, I thought it'd happen quicker, but I guess they have to build up some nerve.

"Oh thank you." I say, and then Patton's right beside me like white on rice, would ya believe.

"Shall we take a walk?" He asks.

I tilt my head to one side because frankly I look adorable when I do that, and then I let him hold the door open for me and we escape outside. The sun is just setting, the sky transformed into a palette of oranges and dusky pinks. We float across to a bench that faces the springs, hear the roar of the water cascading.

"We did it." I say, smiling at Patton. "We cracked the case."

"You've been amazing." He says. "I know I underestimated you at first. I'm sorry."

"Oh, I'm used to it." I say. "People can't believe someone would have this much beauty, and brains."

He laughs.

"It's going to be strange, being seen by people again."

"Damn right it is." Patton agrees as an older woman with a tiny dog in a pushchair walks by, staring at us.

"Good evening." I say and she practically bursts into a run.

"That woman will have my life when she stops being scared." Patton says. "Mrs Jacobson. She's the neighbor from hell. New complaint every week about kids playing soccer near her house and stuff. Once, the ice cream truck was too loud."

"She sounds like a hoot." I say as the woman disappears off towards town, stealing a backwards glance towards us every few steps.

"I've enjoyed spending this time with you, Sage." He says, suddenly serious, and I feel my stomach flip.

"I'm married, you know." I say. I look up at him through my thick lashes, see the disappointment flash across his face before he recovers and smiles.

"Of course." He says. "Is he... is he, here?"

I shake my head. "Married in name only. Things were falling apart when I died."

"I'm sorry to hear that."

"Oh, don't be. Patton, I've been dead a long time." I say with a small laugh. "He's passed too, but we're not together. I mean, we met up when he passed, I went to greet him, but it was pretty clear one life was enough for us to be together."

He nods. "I never settled down."

"Because of work?"

"I guess." He says. "I was pretty ambitious, always wanting to work my way up the ranks to Sheriff and then when I did, wanting to be the best Sheriff I could be."

"You did a great job. Everyone loves you."

He shrugs. "It would have been nice to go home to a woman, ya know?"

I feel my cheeks flush and don't know what to say.

"Sorry, I should..."

"No." I object. "Don't stop talking."

"Okay." He says with a chuckle but then remains silent. The moment has passed and I want to claw it back.

"It is kind of lonely sometimes." I say, my voice small. "I mean, I've got Connie, but she can't spend all her time with the dead, that's not healthy."

"You've got me." Patton says, glancing across at me and braving a small smile.

I nod.

And then a cough comes from behind us.

"So... Mariam and Desiree, hey?" Atticus asks. He gazes at us both.

"Who cares." I say with a shrug. "Happiness is all that matters."

"Yes it is." Patton says, and he takes my hand in his.

**

Connie's on the veranda when I return home, her feet tucked under a blanket, a glass of sweet tea in her hand. Her eyes are open, but I can sense how tired she is.

"You did it." I call out, sitting by her feet on the painted wood.

"We did it." She corrects.

"When did you realise it was him?"

"I had my suspicions when Lola hit Taylor, and then

when Troy told us it was a spirit, it just had to be him. I didn't think getting him to confess would be so easy."

"He thought he was untouchable." I say.

"I think most of us thought that banishing spirits was just a story, not real."

"I didn't think it was real." I admit. "And I doubt Desmond had even heard about it as a possibility."

"What a horrid man he was."

I nod. "Talking of men..."

Connie looks at me.

"I might have just had a moment with Patton." I say, feeling like a teenager girl. I can remember the days when I'd get a love letter passed across to me in class or left in my locker, how I'd race into Connie's bedroom after school and tell her about it in the tiniest detail. How she'd always tolerate my gushing, while never having a similar story to share with me.

"You two seriously need to get a room." She says, pulling the blanket tighter across her. A young couple walk past and raise their hands to wave. When Connie returns the greeting, I do too, and I feel myself begin to return to a community, begin to feel part of the world again.

"He's so handsome." I say.

"He's totally your type." She agrees.

"I don't want to be alone forever." I say, and her head swivels around to me. "I know I have you. But you know what I mean."

"I don't tell you you're beautiful often enough, do I?" She teases.

"Ha ha."

"You know, Sage, I like Patton. I do."

"But?" I ask.

"There isn't a but."

"There's always a but with you." I say. When John Timberlake started walking me home from school, Connie was ready with the warnings. And when Dave Mitchell brought me a red rose and invited me to prom, Connie was there telling me to be careful. It's in-built, like she has no choice. I see the handsome men and feel the butterflies in my stomach while all she can see are the things that could go wrong.

"Can I join you?" A voice calls, and we both look up then.

Nettie looks radiant in a pale yellow tea dress with sandals, her hair is twisted into some kind of intricate up-do and finished with a yellow flower, and her cheekbones could cut through me if she came much closer. At her feet stands a small suitcase.

"Going somewhere?" Connie asks.

Nettie glances at the suitcase then back at us, and she actually looks at both of us. This is going to take some getting used to.

"No way." She says. "These are my things from the jail. I managed to convince Sheriff Morton to return home and pack some of my things after the first night. I'm not going anywhere."

"Have you heard the news?" Connie asks. "I mean, I'm guessing you've been told you're not a suspect any more or you wouldn't be standing here."

"I know my husband was trying to frame me." Nettie says with a tight nod. "He really is the gift that keeps on giving."

"He won't be bothering anyone again." I say.

"I don't think we've met?" Nettie says, and I hear the shake of nerves in her voice.

"I'm Sage. Connie's sister."

"Pleased to meet you." Nettie says. "I just wanted to come across and say thank you. You believed in me."

"I knew you wouldn't do that."

"Oh no." Nettie says. "I hated that girl but I couldn't have killed her."

"Are they reopening Desmond's case?" I ask.

Nettie shakes her head. "I don't think anyone's particularly keen to spend their time on that, not now."

"That must be a relief." Connie says. "You can just move forward with your life now."

"I intend to." Nettie says. She picks up the suitcase and gives us a smile.

THE END

BONUS SHORT STORY

You're read The Ghosts of Mystic Springs!

Now discover what it was like for Sage as she transitioned to the spirit world in this exclusive short story.

This short story is NOT available anywhere else online.

Request your copy now at

http://monamarple.com/MS1

You'll also join my VIP Reader List, and will receive a weekly eMail update every Thursday full of news, special offers and free gifts.

ABOUT THE AUTHOR

Mona Marple is a lover of all things bookish. That's a word, right?

She is happiest when she's either curled up reading an excellent book, or hammering away at her keyboard trying to write one.

She's been creating characters and worlds since she was a child, and never forgets the magic of being able to connect with people through her writing.

If you've enjoyed this book, Mona would love to connect with you.

facebook.com/monamarpleauthor

twitter.com/monamarple

instagram.com/monamarple

ALSO BY MONA MARPLE

Mona Marple is the creator of the Mystic Springs paranormal cozy mystery series and the Waterfell Tweed cozy mystery series.

You can check out all of Mona's books by visiting:

author.to/MonaMarple

Made in the USA
San Bernardino, CA
28 July 2018